THE DOVES' NEST
and Other Stories

Katherine Mansfield

The Doves' Nest
AND OTHER STORIES

Centenary Edition
Introduced by C. A. Hankin

CENTURY HUTCHINSON

This edition published 1988 by
Century Hutchinson New Zealand Ltd
An imprint of the Century Hutchinson Group
187–189 Archers Road, Glenfield, Auckland 10

Century Hutchinson Ltd
62–65 Chandos Place, Covent Garden, London WC2N 4NW

Century Hutchinson Australia Pty. Ltd
16–22 Church Street, Hawthorn, Melbourne, Victoria 3122

Century Hutchinson South Africa Pty. Ltd
P.O. Box 337, Bergvlei 2012, South Africa

ISBN 1-86941-017-3

Design and production by Edsetera Book Productions Ltd
Typesetting processed in Goudy Old Style
by Typocrafters Ltd, Auckland
Printed in Hong Kong

CONTENTS

Biographical Note   7

Introduction   11

The Doll's House   27

The Honeymoon   35

A Cup of Tea   41

Taking the Veil   49

The Fly   55

The Canary   61

A Married Man's Story   65

The Doves' Nest   77

Six Years After   91

Daphne   97

Father and the Girls   103

All Serene!   109

A Bad Idea   115

A Man and His Dog   119

Such a Sweet Old Lady   123

Honesty   125

Susannah   129

Second Violin   133

Mr and Mrs Williams   137

Weak Heart   141

Widowed   145

Select Bibliography   151

BIOGRAPHICAL NOTE

Some two years before she died, Katherine Mansfield outlined in a self-deprecating sketch her career as a writer:

> My literary career began with short-story writing in New Zealand. I was nine years old when my first attempt was published. I have been filling notebooks ever since. After I came to London I worked for some time for the *New Age*, and published *In a German Pension* in 1912. It was a bad book, but the press was kind to it. Later, I worked with my present husband, Mr John Middleton Murry, editor of the *Athenaeum*, but at that time editor of *Rhythm* and the *Blue Review*. In the past two years I have reviewed novels for the *Athenaeum*, and I have written more short stories. Such a prolonged exercise ought to have produced something a great deal better than *Bliss*; I hope the book on which I am now engaged will be more worthy of the interest of the public. It is a collection of stories — one with a New Zealand setting in the style of "Prelude". Several are character sketches of women rather like poor Miss Ada Moss in the story "Pictures".

The personal and emotional life to which Katherine Mansfield here makes little allusion is not so simply summed up. She was born Kathleen Beauchamp on 14 October 1888 in Wellington. Her father, Harold (later Sir Harold) Beauchamp, possibly the most important man in her life, was a prospering businessman, already relentlessly pursuing his goal of wealth and social standing. Kathleen, the middle child in a family of four daughters and a son, grew up in a large, socially active household, which included her warm-hearted maternal grandmother and her then unmarried aunt, Belle Dyer. As an adult writer, Katherine Mansfield was to draw again and again upon the formative first fourteen years of her life spent in Wellington.

In a life that was notable for its numerous changes of residences, Kathleen's first, momentous, physical upheaval occurred in January 1903, when she and her sisters sailed from New Zealand for England and the superior education offered at Queen's College in London. During her three and a half years at that enlightened school, Kathleen's receptive mind was exposed to the latest artistic fashions of the day, including the writings of Walter Pater, Oscar Wilde, Arthur Symons and the French symbolist poets. Perhaps even more important, she cemented what was to be a lifelong friendship with the selfless Ida Baker, known affectionately as L.M.

By the time Kathleen Beauchamp was brought back, in December 1906, from the artistic attractions of London to the comparative dullness of existence in colonial New Zealand, she had become a very rebellious young woman. Determined now to be a writer, she eventually prevailed, in 1908, upon the harassed Harold Beauchamp to send her back to London with an allowance of £100 a year. "The only way to get rid of temptation is to yield to it," she quoted Wilde in her *Journal* in 1906. For the next few years Katherine Mansfield, as she now called herself, did just that, changing lovers almost as frequently as she changed abodes. It was not until 1912, when she and John Middleton Murry began living together, that her emotional life, at least, became somewhat settled.

In London, Katherine Mansfield gradually made her mark as a writer (as did Murry as a critic and editor); and gradually she came to mix with, if not to be completely accepted by, most of the important English literary figures of her time: D. H. Lawrence, Virginia Woolf, Lady Ottoline Morrell, T. S. Eliot, Aldous Huxley, Bertrand Russell and others. During her early years in London, she had been no stranger to personal suffering; but tragedy struck again in 1915 when her only brother, Leslie, was killed in the war. Then, in 1918, after fleeing to France to escape the ravages of an English winter, she herself received what amounted to a death sentence: the diagnosis of pulmonary tuberculosis

In the five years that were left to her, Katherine Mansfield poured out, even as she transformed into art, her physical, mental and emotional anguish in a series of inimitable short stories. She also wrote daily letters — to her friends, but especially to Murry, whom she had married in May 1918. Journeying restlessly back and forth from England to the Continent (particularly France) in search of improved health, Katherine Mansfield endured long separations from Murry. In her loneliness and dependency it was upon the faithful L.M. whom she increasingly leaned.

By 1922 she was searching for the one thing that could save her: a miracle. But Dr Manoukhin, the French physician who claimed to cure tuberculosis by irradiating the spleen, managed only to deplete her purse and exhaust her remaining energy. On 16 October, two days after her thirty-fourth birthday, Katherine Mansfield sought sanctuary, one might say, at the Gurdjieff Institute for the Harmonious Development of Man at Fontainebleau, near Paris. The evidence suggests that here she found a measure of peace before she died of a massive haemorrhage on 9 January 1923.

After her death, John Middleton Murry, inadequate though he may have been as the husband of a dying woman, did not fail Katherine Mansfield the writer. Not without emotional cost to himself, he gradually edited and put before the public two more collections of stories, *The Aloe* (the long first version of "Prelude"), together with her poems, her letters both to himself and others, her *Journal* and her literary criticism. Today, one hundred years after her birth, Katherine Mansfield's reputation as a writer and as a supremely courageous, if fallible, human being is higher than ever she or her contemporaries could have imagined. Never out of print, her writings have at their best a quality of beauty and time-lessness that continues to be a source of strength and delight to succeeding generations of readers.

INTRODUCTION

Katherine Mansfield's fourth collected volume, *The Doves' Nest and Other Stories*, was published posthumously in June 1923. Before illness put an end to her writing, she had chosen the title for her new book and had drawn up a preliminary list of stories for it, some set in London and some in New Zealand. "I have a book to finish," she told a fellow writer in August 1922. Sadly, she was to write no more stories before her death in January 1923, and it was Murry who had finally to decide what to include. In a farewell letter written in August 1922, Katherine gave her husband implicit permission to publish the writing she had left behind. "All my manuscripts I leave entirely to you to do what you like with," she told him. "Go through them one day, dear love, and destroy all you do not use." Accordingly, Murry selected fifteen unfinished pieces to accompany the five new stories Katherine Mansfield had written for the book. *The Doves' Nest* is necessarily an uneven collection; but, as Murry pointed out in his introduction, it does have chronological continuity. All the stories, finished and unfinished, were written at the same time as, or after, the work published in *The Garden-Party and Other Stories* — that is, between July 1921 and July 1922. To read *The Doves' Nest*, especially in conjunction with her letters and *Journal*, is to follow something of Katherine Mansfield's inner journey in the closing eighteen months of her life.

Although Murry later endured a good deal of unjust criticism for publishing his wife's writing posthumously, early reviewers of *The Doves' Nest* found no such fault. Writing in the *London Mercury* in 1923, J. B. Priestley said: "This posthumous volume of Katherine Mansfield's stories is not merely a number of fragments huddled together by an enthusiastic literary executor: it is a volume planned, and even named, by the writer herself, although the greater number of the stories contained in it are unfinished." Of the unfinished pieces he wrote: "even . . . the merest beginnings are capital reading. Even though we never come to the point, and do not know what the stories are *about*, it does not seem to matter very much. The delicate enchantments of her art are there as of old." One story Priestley selected for special comment was "the Doll's House". This, he said, was "a little gem".

By general consensus, two stories in *The Doves' Nest* — "The Doll's House" and "The Fly" — stand out as being among Katherine Mansfield's major achievements in the art of the short story. It is surely no accident that these two works are solidly based in the New Zealand of the author's girlhood. Coincidentally, "The Doll's House", written between 24 and 30 October 1921, was published in the *Nation* on 4 February 1922 — the same day as her other famous New Zealand story, "The Garden-Party", was published in the *Westminster Gazette*. Both these stories reflect Katherine Mansfield's rejection of the barriers artificially raised among human beings by class distinctions and social snobbery. But while "The Garden-Party" is set at 75 Tinakori Road in Karori, the home Katherine Mansfield knew as an adolescent, "The Doll's House" shares with "Prelude" the setting of her earlier childhood home, "Chesney Wold". It shares, too, many of the cast of "Prelude": the three Burnell children (Isabel, Lottie and Kezia), Aunt Beryl and Pat, the handyman. Absent, however, is the father, Stanley Burnell; and the children's mother appears only as an authoritative adult voice.

In September 1921 when she was making a note of stories for her new book, Katherine listed "The Doll's House" as "The Washer-woman's Children" and gives a version of the closing lines: "'The little lamp I seen it.' And then they were silent." A much earlier *Journal* entry indicates, however, that the inspiration for the story goes back to 1916 when Katherine Mansfield was working on the first draft of "Prelude". In the notes she made then, her memory of the actual doll's house that was given to the Beauchamp children was interwoven with emotionally powerful feelings about being displaced as a toddler in the affections of her mother and grandmother by a sickly new baby, Gwen. "My mother paid no attention to me at all", Katherine remembered. She also recalled asking grandmother when Gwen would play with the new doll's house: "Mrs Heywood had just given us the doll's house. It was a beautiful one with a verandah and a balcony and a door that opened and shut and two chimneys. I wanted badly to show it to someone."

Kathleen Beauchamp had a sense of proprietorship over the new doll's house because her two older sisters had been sent away before it arrived, "so that was why I so longed to have somebody to show it to. I had gone all through it myself, from the kitchen to the dining-room, up into the bedrooms with the doll's lamp on the table, heaps and heaps of times. '*When* will she play with it?'

I asked grandmother." But even the doll's house hardly made up for the fact that

> all day, all night grandmother's arms were full. I had no lap to climb into, no pillow to rest against. All belonged to Gwen. . . .
>
> Down in the kitchen one day old Mrs McElvie came to the door and asked Bridget about the poor little mite, and Bridget said, "Kep' alive on bullock's blood hotted in a saucer over a candle." After that I felt frightened of Gwen, and I decided that even when she did play with the doll's house I would not let her go upstairs into the bedroom — only downstairs, and then only when I saw she could look.

Little Gwen lived only three months, but in that time, a photo was taken. "The picture was hung over the nursery fire," Katherine recalled. "I thought it looked very nice. The doll's house was in it — verandah and balcony and all. Gran held me up to kiss my little sister."

In October 1921, when she transformed these memories into "The Doll's House", Katherine Mansfield rearranged the parts played by the members of her family. It is the bossy eldest sister, Isabel (modelled on Vera Beauchamp), who officiates at the showing-off of the new acquisition. Kezia, the author's fictional self, hovers anxiously in the background; and outside the charmed circle altogether are the two little Kelvey sisters. Many of the story's external details, however, Katherine took directly from life. Mrs Heywood merely becomes "Mrs Hay", and Mrs McElvie who had inquired about baby Gwen is the mother of the spurned "Kelvey" girls. The real Mrs McKelvey was the well-liked village washerwoman in Karori, although her husband, a gardener, was not in prison. An early biographer writes that of the three McKelvey children, "Lil, the eldest, was the only normal one. . . . 'Our Else', the artistic one, was the mother's favourite. . . . They all looked after her. This 'pathetic little wish-bone of a child' cared only for the one thing: she loved to paint."

If "The Doll's House" is one of Katherine Mansfield's most realistic stories, it is because the social attitudes permeating the work were also drawn from the author's childhood memories. When she started school, there was only one primary school in the district, which the children of rich and poor alike attended. The ill-dressed little McKelveys who trailed daily past the gate of the Beauchamps' big house were at the bottom of the social pecking order. A little higher up the scale were the Monaghans, who, like the Logans in the story, kept cows. The adult Katherine Mansfield remembered being tormented by the rough Monaghans. "To me," she wrote to Murry, "it's just as though I'd been going home from school and the Monaghans called after me, and you — about the size of a sixpence — had defended me and p'raps helped me to pick up my pencils and put them back in the pencil box." Lena Monaghan was the model for the spiteful Lena Logan who so cruelly taunts the Kelvey girls. Even the fictional teacher, who encouraged social distinctions by having "a special voice for [the Kelveys] and a special smile for the other children when Lil Kelvey came up to her desk with a bunch of dreadfully common-looking flowers", was based on the actual teacher who was an unpleasant snob. For all its parallels with real life, however, "The Doll's House" is raised far above the level of social commentary by the perception Katherine Mansfield expressed to Dorothy Brett in March 1921: "Beauty triumphs over ugliness in Life. That's what I feel. And that marvellous triumph is what I long to express."

"The Doll's House" was written in Montana where Katherine, who had been joined by Murry, enjoyed a few last months of relative stability in the bracing climate of the Swiss Alps. Among the unfinished stories that belong to this period is "Susannah". "Now for Susannah" reads a *Journal* entry for July 1922. The interest of this fragment lies in its attempt to recreate as fiction an episode from the same period of the author's life as "The Doll's House". As in that story, there are two well-behaved older sisters and a younger, more independently minded child, Susannah. The Heywoods, who had presented the Beauchamps' doll's house, appear as "the Heywoods" whose governess the three children share. Instead of playing with a doll's house, however, Susannah and her sisters enjoy the treat of having "a real tea in the doll's tea set on the table". Katherine Mansfield was probably unable to finish this story because at its heart was a theme she had attempted earlier but had never resolved satisfactorily in art: her own troubled relations with her father. In "Susannah", the children's "kind generous Father" has been persuaded to buy them each a treat — a ticket to the circus. But in a manner reminiscent of the 1912 stories, "New Dresses" and "The Little Girl", Susannah incurs her parents' wrath. She doesn't want to go to the circus. Threatened with punishment for being "a naughty, ungrateful child", Susannah "looked as though she was going to bow down, to bow down to the ground, before her kind generous Father and beg for his forgiveness".

Katherine Mansfield's relations with her father were very much on her mind towards the end of her life. In November 1921 she wrote him a long letter begging, as Susannah had done, for his forgiveness. The parallels between the end of the unfinished story and the letter are striking. "I am ashamed to ask for your forgiveness and yet how can I approach you without it?" she wrote. "Sometimes night after night I dream that I am back in New Zealand and sometimes you are angry with me and at other times this horrible behaviour of mine has not happened and all is well between us." The reason for her silence, she painfully explains, is that she has heard that he begrudges paying her allowance. "But I cannot bear it any longer," the letter concludes. "I must come to you and at least acknowledge my fault. . . . Father don't turn away from me, darling."

Whatever Katherine Mansfield might say to his face, her writing leaves little doubt that at heart she considered her father to be less than generous to her, essentially unforgiving and inordinately self-centred. Some of these feelings are expressed in another unfinished story, "Six Years After", written in November 1921, shortly after the letter which is as much a plea for help as for forgiveness. The man who appears as the impatient Mr Hammond in "The Stranger", and as the self-satisfied Stanley Burnell in "Prelude" and "At the Bay", is in "Six Years After" the domineering husband travelling on a steamer with his acquiescent wife. "He knew, of course, that she ought to be down in the cabin; he knew it was no afternoon for her to be sitting on deck, in this cold and raw mist . . . and he realised how she must be hating it. But he had come to believe that it really was easier for her to make these sacrifices than it was for him." A reference to the wife's "high sealskin collar" suggests that Katherine Mansfield was thinking of her mother as she wrote. For in a 1922 letter to her father recalling the family's 1903 steamer voyage to England, she said: "How I should love to make a long sea voyage again . . . but I always connect such experiences with a vision of Mother in her little sealskin jacket with the collar turned up. I can see her as I write."

The fact that "Six Years After" was twice listed in Katherine Mansfield's *Journal* for inclusion in *The Doves' Nest* indicates its importance to her. "A husband and wife on board a steamer. The cold buttons. They see someone who reminds them," she noted in October 1921. There is, in fact, an other-worldly quality to the story as it develops into the wife's hallucination that she is communing with the spirit of her dead son. Imagining him calling her

15

reproachfully, the anguished mother answers: "I am coming as fast as I can! As fast as I can!" Significantly, it was six years since Katherine's brother, Leslie, had been killed in the war; and she, like the mother in the story, was anticipating following him in death. Writing to Dorothy Brett at this time of her need for a miracle, she added: "[The wind] brings nothing but memories — and by memories I mean those that one cannot without pain remember. It always carries my brother back to me. Ah, Brett, I hope with all my heart that you have not known anyone who has died young — long before their time. It is bitterness."

In desperate search of the only thing that could now save her own life — a miracle — Katherine Mansfield abandoned the peace of Montana in January 1922 for Paris and the expensive, unproven X-ray treatment of Dr Manoukhin. "He promises to cure me by the summer. . . ." she wrote to a friend. "The only fly in the ointment is the terrific expense. It's 300 francs a time. However, I have been fortunate in my work lately and I'll just have to do a double dose of it until this is paid off." Of the seven stories that she said were sitting "on the doorstep", however, Katherine managed to complete only one, "The Fly". On 26 February 1922 she reported to Dorothy Brett: "I have just finished a queer story called 'The Fly'. About a fly that falls into an inkpot and a Bank Manager."

"The Fly" was Katherine Mansfield's last great story, the product at once of her searing physical experiences at the hands of Dr Manoukhin and her tortured feelings for her father. In this consummate work of art, she was finally able to express attitudes towards him — and her dead brother — that she could not bring to a conclusion in "Six Years After". Later she admitted to William Gerhardi, "I hated writing it". Coldly calculating in its objectivity, the story in no way betrays the pent-up hatred that surely contributed to its composition. "Oh, my *hatred*!" Katherine had written on the draft of "Six Years After". Then in January she told her friend Koteliansky, "I have been in a horrible black mood lately, with feelings of something like hatred towards 'everybody'." On 9 February she noted in her *Journal*: "I must not forget the long talk Ida and I had the other evening about *hate*. What is hate? Who has ever described it?"

"The Fly", perhaps more than any other story by Katherine Mansfield, has fascinated and tantalised generations of readers. Although rich in symbolic meanings, this work can also be linked with the author's personal circumstances. The central character in "The Fly" is a bank manager who, six years after the death of his son, can no longer weep for him. Katherine Mansfield's father was the influential chairman of the Bank of New Zealand whose only son and heir had been dead for six years. Katherine Mansfield, battling for breath, was like the fly which grew more feeble after each heroic attempt to save itself from drowning. She had once described her father as "a kind of vast symbolic chapeau out of which I shall draw the little piece of paper that will decide my Fate". In the sadistic character of "the Boss", she created a God-like figure who had the prerogative of mercy but would show none.

"The Fly" and "The Doll's House" are the last major stories that Katherine Mansfield wrote with New Zealand settings. Shortly before leaving Montana she had, however, completed one other work which takes place imaginatively in the New Zealand of her girlhood: "Taking the Veil". "Wrote and finished 'Taking the Veil'," she noted in her *Journal* on 24 January

> It took me about 3 hours to write finally. But I had been thinking over the *decor* and so on for weeks — nay, months, I believe. I can't say how thankful I am to have been born in N.Z., to know Wellington as I do, and to have it to range about in. Writing about the convent seemed so natural. I suppose I have not been in the grounds more than twice. But it is one of the places that remains as vivid as ever.

"Taking the Veil" is a much gentler story than "The Fly". Here death, juxtaposed to young love, is not a fast-approaching reality but a fantasy no sooner entertained than dismissed. There is a tinge of sentiment in the young heroine's daydream of entering a convent, and dying there in the cause of an impossible love; there is also, in the story's ending, a kind of symbolic death and resurrection.

In August 1921, Katherine wrote to Dorothy Brett: "Two nuns have just come with needlework made by infants in their convent. The dear creatures (I have such a romantic *love* of nuns) my two gentle columbines, blue-hooded, mild, folded over . . ." This visit probably suggested "Taking the Veil", since the nuns in that story, which is set in the grounds of the Hill Street convent, near the Beauchamps' Tinakori Road house, also wear blue robes. The emotional inspiration for the work, however, may well have been Walter de la Mare's *The Veil and Other Poems*. The same month that she wrote the story, Katherine told Ottoline Morrell:

I am so glad you like *The Veil*. There is one poem:

> Why has the rose faded and fallen
> And these eyes have not seen. . . .

It haunts me. But it is a state of mind I know so terribly well — That regret for what one has not seen and felt — for what has passed by — unheeded. Life is only given once and then I *waste* it. Do you feel that?

In the months before leaving Montana, Katherine Mansfield began several other stories with New Zealand settings that she was unable to finish: "Honesty" in July, "Second Violin" in August, "Daphne" in November, and "Weak Heart". The latter she seems to have begun in September and taken up again in November. "Today I began to write, seriously, 'The Weak Heart', — a story which fascinates me *deeply*," she noted in her *Journal* on 21 November.

> What I feel it needs so peculiarly is a very subtle variation of "tense" from the present to the past and back again — and softness, lightness, and the feeling that all is in bud, with a play of humour over the character of Ronnie. And the feeling of the Thorndon Baths, the wet, moist, oozy . . . no, I know how it must be done.

In terms of Katherine Mansfield's emotional life, "Weak Heart" can be linked with "Six Years After", also begun and abandoned that month. But whereas the latter fragment is a poignant reminder of the premature death of Leslie Beauchamp, "Weak Heart" ends with the shock to a brother when his gifted young sister dies. Katherine, who had been very musical as a girl, played the piano in Montana. It is not hard to see her, who always believed she had a weak heart, imaginatively transposing her fate onto the musical Edie Bengel whose piano rings out: "Ah, if life must pass so quickly, why is the breath of these flowers so sweet? What is the meaning of this feeling of longing, of such sweet trouble — of flying joy? Goodbye! Farewell!"

Katherine Mansfield's last stories reflect her preoccupation with death; but she also continued to explore the relationship between married couples. The most notable work in *The Doves' Nest* on the subject of marriage is the long, unfinished "A Married Man's Story", now known to have been written in August 1921. (Although Murry in his introduction correctly ascribed the story to the Montana period, biographers have until recently assumed that it was written in the summer of 1918, shortly after the Murrys' marriage.) The married man, who narrates his own story, is a cynical, self-confessed liar who no longer loves his wife, now a "broken-hearted woman". The question around which his monologue twists and turns is "why do people stay together?" His answer is that they are bound by "their secret relation to each other" which even they can hardly understand. Proposing to write "the plain truth, as only a liar can write it", he admits that "until last autumn" he and his wife had been "radiantly happy".

Marriage was very much on Katherine's mind in the period preceding the story's composition — that is, in the autumn of 1921. "What is happening to married pairs?" she asked Sylvia Lynd in September.

> They are almost extinct. I confess, for my part, I believe in marriage. It seems to me the only possible relation that really is satisfying. And how else is one to have peace of mind to enjoy life and to do one's work? To know *one other* seems to me a far greater adventure than to be on kissing acquaintance with dear knows how many. It certainly takes a lifetime and it's far more "wonderful" as times goes on. . . . People nowadays seem to live in such confusion. I have a horror of dark muddles.

Her own marriage had gone by no means smoothly since the autumn of 1920. Then, having returned to Menton with L. M., she became increasingly jealous of Murry's flirtations in London with other women. Dorothy Brett annoyed Katherine with tactless letters about enjoying tennis with Murry; but even more wounding was his admitted friendship with Princess Elizabeth Bibesco. About this time, Katherine made a *Journal* entry that both reflects her feelings and reads almost as a preliminary note for "A Married Man's Story":

> I thought, a few minutes ago, that I could have written a whole novel about a *Liar*. A man who was devoted to his wife, but who lied. But I couldn't. I couldn't write a whole novel about anything. I suppose I shall write stories about it. But at this moment I can't get through to anything. There's something like a wall of sand between me and the whole of my "world". I feel as though I am *dirty* or *disgusted* or both.

But as Katherine Mansfield once told a friend, she was always "renewing a marriage" with Murry. By August 1921, when he was safely at her side in Montana, she could contemplate objectively the relationship between lovers: "We are neither male nor female.

We are a compound of both. I choose the male who will develop and expand the male in me; he chooses me to expand the female in him." Put slightly differently in the words of the fictional married man, "It is . . . the second self . . . who makes the choice for his own particular purposes, and . . . it's the second self in the other which responds."

In virtually all the stories in *The Doves' Nest* on the subject of marriage, there is the suggestion of an underlying insecurity beneath the wife's surface happiness. " Widowed", also begun in August 1921, is about a self-satisfied young wife whose husband is suddenly killed in an accident; in "All Serene", written in November, the husband appears to be a deceiver of his wife, as does the male narrator of "A Bad Idea", started some time after February 1922. Rather different in emphasis is "A Cup of Tea", which was written on 11 January in "about 4–5 hours". (Murry wrote to Katherine in Paris: "Cassells have bought 'A Cup of Tea' for ten guineas and that's exactly the kind of story they want.") Here, the charity shown a penniless London girl by the rich and selfish Rosemary Fell turns into jealousy when her husband remarks upon the other woman's good looks. "Mr and Mrs Williams", a fragment probably written in late January or early February, is much less serious in tone. Mr and Mrs Williams are preparing to splash out on a holiday in Switzerland, thanks to a legacy from old Aunt Aggie, happily released "after fifteen years in a wheel-chair". Katherine Mansfield's wicked sense of humour shines out in a letter she wrote to William Gerhardi about the story on 8 February:

> By the way, for proof of *your* being a writer you had only to mention a bath chair and it crept into your handwriting. It was a queer coincidence. I had just been writing about a bath chair myself and poor old Aunt Aggie, who had lived in one and died in one — *glided* off, so that one saw her in her purple velvet steering carefully among the stars and whimpering faintly as was her terrestrial wont when the wheel jolted over a particularly large one. But these conveyances are not to be taken lightly or wantonly. They are terrible things.

Katherine wrote "Honeymoon", one final, thought-provoking story about marriage, in late March or early April 1922. Fanny and George are radiantly happy honeymooning on the Mediterranean; but their very different reactions to the quavering voice of an ageing singer betray the seeds of future disharmony.

A sense of urgency about her writing enters Katherine Mansfield's letters in the early part of 1922. Needing the money from her stories to pay for the costly Manoukhin treatment, she often found herself too exhausted to work. "I'll have to write at least a story a week until next May, which is a little bit frightening," she told Gerhardi. By March she was admitting to Dorothy Brett: "What is a nuisance is I can*not* work for the moment and Shorter has ordered thirteen stories, all at one go, to be ready in July. So there they are in addition to my ordinary work." As she struggled to put a brave face on her increasing physical helplessness in an essentially indifferent world, Katherine's imagination turned towards a group of people whose plight was not dissimilar to her own: ageing individuals with little to look forward to. Two fragmentary pieces about old age, "A Man and His Dog" and "Such a Sweet Old Lady", were begun some time after February 1922.

In June she left Paris to recuperate from the X-ray treatment at Sierre. There, during June and July, she worked on two more unfinished stories, "The Doves' Nest" and "Father and the Girls", and completed her last story, "The Canary". She started "The Doves' Nest", planned as a long narrative work in the gently humorous vein of "Daughters of the Late Colonel", in January 1922. "Wrote 'the Doves' Nest' this afternoon," she noted in her *Journal*. "I was in no mood to write, it seemed impossible. Yet when I had finished three pages they were 'all right'. This is a proof (never to be too often proved) that once one has thought out a story nothing remains but the *labour*." On 9 January she told Dorothy Brett: "I'm working at such a big story that I still can only just see the end in my imagination . . . the longest by far I've ever written. It's called *The Doves' Nest*. But winter is a bad black time for work, I think. One's brain gets congealed. It is very hard." On 20 January she mentioned the story again to Brett: "However, I swear to finish my big story by the end of this month. It's queer when I am in this mood I always write as though I am laughing. I feel it running along the pages. If only the reader could see the snail in its shell with the black pen!" Laughter imbues this narrative about the efforts of the widowed Mrs Fawcett, sojourning with her daughter, Milly, in the South of France, to charm a visiting American. This was a story that Katherine Mansfield obviously enjoyed writing. She took it up again in June, when she wrote to Gerhardi.

I am in the middle of a very long story written in the same style

— horrible expression! — as *The Daughters of the Late Colonel*. I enjoy writing it so much that even after I am asleep, I go on. The scene is the South of France in early spring. There is a real love story in it, too, and rain, buds, frogs, a thunderstorm, pink spotted Chinese dragons. There is no happiness greater than this leading a *double life*. But it's mysterious, too. How is it possible to be here in this remote, deserted hotel and at the same time to be leaning out of the window of the Villa Martin listening to the rain thrumming so gently on the leaves and smelling the night-scented stocks with Milly? (I shall be awfully disappointed if you don't like Milly.)

Unfortunately, what promised to be a major work did not flow fast enough. Katherine told Murry in early August: "once 'The Doves' Nest' is finished I shall leave here. It will take a fortnight, not a week"; but it was still incomplete when she and L.M. left Switzerland for London on 16 August.

Of the stories that Katherine Mansfield worked on during that last sojourn in Sierre, one — "Father and the Girls" — was inspired by the hotel Château Belle Vue where she was staying. On 29 July 1922, in a deceptively lively letter to her father, she described the fellow guests who were the models for "Father and the Girls":

There is a remarkable old talker here at present — an American, aged eighty-eight — with his wife and daughter. The daughter looks about sixty-five. According to the ancient gentleman, they have been on the wing ever since he retired at the age of seventy-five, and they intend remaining on the wing for another fifteen years or so!

In her story, the father, who has an American accent ("Sims to me a nice room. . . . Do you girls wanna change it?"), is eighty-four. Instead of travelling with a wife and daughter, he has two daughters: "As for Edith and Emily — well he looked more like their elder brother". Father travels ceaselessly because he is afraid of staying at home, "fixed in one place as if waiting for somebody or something".

In "The Canary", the elderly female narrator *is* confined to her lonely little house with only a canary for companionship. Although Katherine Mansfield wrote the story for Dorothy Brett on 7 July while Brett was staying with her in Sierre, "The Canary" had been in gestation since February. Thanking a friend for the address of the Victoria Palace Hotel in Paris, Katherine added: "I have . . . a view into the windows opposite — which I love. It's so nice to watch la belle dame opposite bring her canary *in* when it rains and put the·hyacinth *out*." The canary opposite had already become a potential story by 26 February, when Katherine wrote to Brett:

> I think my story for you will be called *Canaries*. The large cage opposite has fascinated me completely. I think and think about them — their feelings, their *dreams*, the life they led before they were caught, the difference between the two little pale fluffy ones who were born in captivity and their grandfather and grandmother who knew the South American forests and have seen the immense perfumed sea. . . . Words cannot express the beauty of that high shrill little song rising out of the very stone. . . .

It is somehow fitting that Katherine Mansfield's last complete story is a celebration of the non-human, natural world that gave her such solace. But "The Canary" is also a lament for the inescapable pain of life itself. The plaintive words of the lonely woman grieving for her dead canary, "there does seem something sad in life", might well be the author's. "It is incredible . . . how mysterious and isolated we each of us are — at the last," Katherine had written to Ottoline Morrell. "I suppose one ought to make this discovery once and for all, but I seem to be always making it again." By 7 August, Katherine Mansfield's intimations of mortality were such that she took her final leave of Murry in a letter to be opened after her death. A few days later she rejected an invitation to travel with her father, who had come to England, because "there is always the feeling that I may be doing the very thing that will send me on my last journey before my work is anything like finished here below!"

But her work *was* finished. Hardly able to walk in London, she returned to Paris in October on a quest that was more spiritual than physical. "I have to die to so much," she wrote to Murry. "I have to make such *big* changes. I feel the only thing to do is to get the dying over — to court it, almost." As to her writing — "I do not want to write any stories until I am a less terribly poor human being," she told Koteliansky. Having made her solitary decision to enter the Gurdjieff Institute, Katherine wrote to Murry about her failure to find a physical cure:

> The miracle never came near happening. It couldn't, Boge. And as for my spirit — well, as a result of that life at the Victoria

Palace I stopped being a writer. I have only written long or short scraps since *The Fly*. If I had gone on with my old life I never would have written again, for I was dying of poverty of life.

From Fontainebleau she repeated that she could write no more stories: "As for writing stories and 'being true to one's gift', I couldn't write them if I were not here, even. I am at an end of my source for the time. Life has brought me no *flow*. I want to write, but differently — far more steadily."

In October 1920, Katherine Mansfield had assured Murry: "If I believed at this moment I was going to die, of course I would say 'Come!' because it would be unbearable not — to have you to see me off on the journey where you know the train drops into a great black hole." She was true to her word. On 31 December 1922, the same day as she bade farewell to her cousin, Elizabeth von Arnim, Katherine wrote asking her husband to visit her at Fontainebleau. He arrived on 9 January 1923 and that night she died.

Cherry Hankin
University of Canterbury
Christchurch

THE DOVES' NEST
and Other Stories

The Doll's House

WHEN DEAR OLD MRS HAY went back to town after staying with the Burnells she sent the children a doll's house. It was so big that the carter and Pat carried it into the courtyard, and there it stayed, propped up on two wooden boxes beside the feed-room door. No harm could come to it; it was summer. And perhaps the smell of paint would have gone off by the time it had to be taken in. For, really, the smell of paint coming from that doll's house ("Sweet of old Mrs Hay, of course; most sweet and generous!") — but the smell of paint was quite enough to make anyone seriously ill, in Aunt Beryl's opinion. Even before the sacking was taken off. And when it was . . .

There stood the doll's house, a dark, oily, spinach green, picked out with bright yellow. Its two solid little chimneys, glued on to the roof, were painted red and white, and the door, gleaming with yellow varnish, was like a little slab of toffee. Four windows, real windows, were divided into panes by a broad streak of green. There was actually a tiny porch, too, painted yellow, with big lumps of congealed paint hanging along the edge.

But perfect, perfect little house! Pat prised it open with his pen-knife, and the whole house front swung back, and — there you were, gazing at one and the same moment into the drawing-room and dining-room, the kitchen and two bedrooms. That is the way for a house to open! Why don't all houses open like that? How much more exciting than peering through the slit of a door into a mean little hall with a hat-stand and two umbrellas! That is — isn't it? — what you long to know about a house when you put your hand on the knocker. Perhaps it is the way God opens houses at the dead of night when He is taking a quiet turn with an angel. . . .

"Oh-oh!" The Burnell children sounded as though they were in despair. It was too marvellous; it was too much for them. They had never seen anything like it in their lives. All the rooms were papered. There were pictures on the walls, painted on the paper, with gold frames complete. Red carpet covered all the floors except the kitchen; red plush chairs in the drawing-room, green in the dining-room; tables, beds with real bedclothes, a cradle, a stove, a dresser with tiny plates and one big jug. But what Kezia liked more than anything, what she liked frightfully, was the lamp. It stood in the middle of the dining-room table, an exquisite little amber lamp with a white globe. It was even filled all ready for lighting, though of course, you couldn't light it. But there was something inside that looked like oil and moved when you shook it.

The father and mother dolls, who sprawled very stiff as though they had fainted in the drawing-room, and their two little children asleep upstairs, were really too big for the doll's house. They didn't look as though they belonged. But the lamp was perfect. It seemed to smile at Kezia, to say, "I live here." The lamp was real.

The Burnell children could hardly walk to school fast enough the next morning. They burned to tell everybody, to describe to — well — to boast about their doll's house before the school-bell rang.

"I'm to tell," said Isabel, "because I'm the eldest. And you two can join in after. But I'm to tell first."

There was nothing to answer. Isabel was bossy, but she was always right, and Lottie and Kezia knew too well the powers that went with being eldest. They brushed through the thick buttercups at the road edge and said nothing.

"And I'm to choose who's to come and see it first. Mother said I might."

For it had been arranged that while the doll's house stood in the courtyard they might ask the girls at school, two at a time, to come and look. Not to stay to tea, of course, or to come traipsing through the house. But just to stand quietly in the courtyard while Isabel pointed out the beauties, and Lottie and Kezia looked pleased. . . .

But hurry as they might, by the time they had reached the tarred palings of the boys' playground the bell had begun to jangle. They only just had time to whip off their hats and fall into line before the roll was called. Never mind. Isabel tried to make up for it by looking very important and mysterious and by whispering behind her hand to the girls near her, "Got something to tell you at playtime."

Playtime came and Isabel was surrounded. The girls of her class nearly fought to put their arms round her, to walk away with her, to beam flatteringly, to be her special friend. She held quite a court under the huge pine trees at the side of the playground. Nudging, giggling together, the little girls pressed up close. And the only two who stayed outside the ring were the two who were always outside, the little Kelveys. They knew better than to come anywhere near the Burnells.

For the fact was, the school the Burnell children went to was not at all the kind of place their parents would have chosen if there had been any choice. But there was none. It was the only school for miles. And the consequence was all the children of the neighbourhood, the Judge's little girls, the doctor's daughters, the storekeeper's children, the milkman's, were forced to mix together. Not to speak of there being an equal number of rude, rough little boys as well. But the line had to be drawn somewhere. It was drawn at the Kelveys. Many of the children, including the Burnells, were not allowed even to speak to them. They walked past the Kelveys with their heads in the air, and as they set the fashion in all matters of behaviour, the Kelveys were shunned by everybody. Even the teacher had a special voice for them, and a special smile for the other children when Lil Kelvey came up to her desk with a bunch of dreadfully common-looking flowers.

They were the daughters of a spry, hard-working little washerwoman, who went about from house to house by the day. This was awful enough. But where was Mr Kelvey? Nobody knew for certain. But everybody said he was in prison. So they were the daughters of a washerwoman and a jailbird. Very nice company for other people's children! And they looked it. Why Mrs Kelvey made them so conspicuous was hard to understand. The truth was they were dressed in "bits" given to her by the people for whom she worked. Lil, for instance, who was a stout, plain child, with big freckles, came to school in a dress made from a green art-serge tablecloth of the Burnells', with red plush sleeves from the Logans' curtains. Her hat, perched on top of her high forehead, was a grown-up woman's hat, once the property of Miss Lecky, the postmistress. It was turned up at the back and trimmed with a large scarlet quill. What a little guy she looked! It was impossible not to laugh. And her little sister, our Else, wore a long white dress, rather like a nightgown, and a pair of little boy's boots. But whatever our Else wore she would have looked strange. She was a tiny wishbone of a child, with cropped hair and enormous solemn eyes — a little white owl. Nobody had ever seen her smile; she scarcely ever spoke. She went through life holding on to Lil, with a piece of Lil's skirt screwed up in her hand. Where Lil went, our Else followed. In the playground, on the road going to and from school, there was Lil marching in front and our Else holding on behind. Only when she wanted anything, or when she was out of breath, our Else gave Lil a tug, a twitch, and Lil stopped and turned round. The Kelveys never failed to understand each other.

Now they hovered at the edge; you couldn't stop them listening. When the little girls turned round and sneered, Lil, as usual, gave her silly, shamefaced smile, but our Else only looked.

And Isabel's voice, so very proud, went on telling. The carpet made a great sensation, but so did the beds with real bedclothes, and the stove with an oven door.

When she finished Kezia broke in. "You've forgotten the lamp, Isabel."

"Oh yes," said Isabel, "and there's a teeny little lamp, all made of yellow glass, with a white glove that stands on the dining-room table. You couldn't tell it from a real one."

"The lamp's best of all," cried Kezia. She thought Isabel wasn't making half enough of the little lamp. But nobody paid any attention. Isabel was choosing the two who were to come back with them that afternoon and see it. She chose Emmie Cole and Lena Logan. But when the others knew they were all to have a chance, they couldn't be nice enough to Isabel. One by one they put their arms round Isabel's waist and walked her off. They had something to whisper to her, a secret. "Isabel's *my* friend."

Only the little Kelveys moved away forgotten; there was nothing more for them to hear.

Days passed, and as more children saw the doll's house, the fame of it spread. It became the one subject, the rage. The one question was, "Have you seen Burnells' doll's house? Oh, ain't it lovely!" "Haven't you seen it? Oh, I say!"

Even the dinner hour was given up to talking about it. The little girls sat under the pines eating their thick mutton sandwiches and big slabs of johnny cake spread with butter. While always, as near as they could get, sat the Kelveys, our Else holding on to Lil, listening too, while they chewed their jam sandwiches out of a newspaper soaked with large red blobs.

"Mother," said Kezia, "can't I ask the Kelveys just once?"

"Certainly not, Kezia."

"But why not?"

"Run away, Kezia; you know quite well why not."

At last everybody had seen it except them. On that day the subject rather flagged. It was the dinner hour. The children stood together under the pine trees, and suddenly, as they looked at the Kelveys eating out of their paper, always by themselves, always listening, they wanted to be horrid to them. Emmie Cole started the whisper.

"Lil Kelvey's going to be a servant when she grows up."

"O-oh, how awful!" said Isabel Burnell, and she made eyes at Emmie.

Emmie swallowed in a very meaning way and nodded to Isabel as she'd seen her mother do on those occasions.

"It's true — it's true — it's true," she said.

Then Lena Logan's little eyes snapped. "Shall I ask her?" she whispered.

"Bet you don't," said Jessie May.

"Pooh, I'm not frightened," said Lena. Suddenly she gave a little squeal and danced in front of the other girls. "Watch! Watch me! Watch me now!" said Lena. And sliding, gliding, dragging one foot, giggling behind her hand, Lena went over to the Kelveys.

Lil looked up from her dinner. She wrapped the rest quickly away. Our Else stopped chewing. What was coming now?

"Is it true you're going to be a servant when you grow up, Lil Kelvey?" shrilled Lena.

Dead silence. But instead of answering, Lil only gave her silly, shamefaced smile. She didn't seem to mind the question at all. What a sell for Lena! The girls began to titter.

Lena couldn't stand that. She put her hands on her hips; she shot forward. "Yah, yer father's in prison!" she hissed spitefully.

This was such a marvellous thing to have said that the little girls rushed away in a body, deeply, deeply excited, wild with joy. Someone found a long rope, and they began skipping. And never did they skip so high, run in and out so fast, or do such daring things as on that morning.

In the afternoon Pat called for the Burnell children with the buggy and they drove home. There were visitors. Isabel and Lottie, who liked visitors, went upstairs to change their pinafores. But Kezia thieved out at the back. Nobody was about; she began to swing on the big white gates of the courtyard. Presently, looking along the road, she saw two little dots. They grew bigger, they were coming towards her. Now she could see that one was in front and one close behind. Now she could see that they were the Kelveys. Kezia stopped swinging. She slipped off the gate as if she was going to run away. Then she hesitated. The Kelveys came nearer, and beside them walked their shadows, very long, stretching right across the road with their heads in the buttercups. Kezia clambered back on the gate; she had made up her mind; she swung out.

"Hullo," she said to the passing Kelveys.

They were so astounded that they stopped. Lil gave her silly smile. Our Else stared.

"You can come and see our doll's house if you want to," said Kezia, and she dragged one toe on the ground. But at that Lil turned red and shook her head quickly.

"Why not?" asked Kezia.

Lil gasped, then she said, "Your ma told our ma you wasn't to speak to us."

"Oh, well," said Kezia. She didn't know what to reply. "It doesn't matter. You can come and see our doll's house all the same. Come on. Nobody's looking."

But Lil shook her head still harder.

"Don't you want to?" asked Kezia.

Suddenly there was a twitch, a tug at Lil's skirt. She turned round. Our Else was looking at her with big, imploring eyes; she was frowning; she wanted to go. For a moment Lil looked at our Else very doubtfully. But then our Else twitched her skirt again. She started forward. Kezia led the way. Like two little stray cats they followed across the courtyard to where the doll's house stood.

"There it is," said Kezia.

There was a pause. Lil breathed loudly, almost snorted; our Else was still as stone.

"I'll open it for you," said Kezia kindly. She undid the hook and they looked inside.

"There's the drawing-room and the dining-room, and that's the —"

"Kezia!"

Oh, what a start they gave!

"Kezia!"

It was Aunt Beryl's voice. They turned round. At the back door stood Aunt Beryl, staring as if she couldn't believe what she saw.

"How dare you ask the little Kelveys into the courtyard!" said her cold, furious voice. "You know as well as I do, you're not allowed to talk to them. Run away, children, run away at once. And don't come back again," said Aunt Beryl. And she stepped into the yard and shooed them out as if they were chickens.

"Off you go immediately!" she called, cold and proud.

They did not need telling twice. Burning with shame, shrinking together, Lil huddling along like her mother, our Else dazed, somehow they crossed the big courtyard and squeezed through the white gate.

"Wicked, disobedient little girl!" said Aunt Beryl bitterly to Kezia, and she slammed the doll's house to.

The afternoon had been awful. A letter had come from Willie Brent, a terrifying, threatening letter, saying if she did not meet him that evening in Pulman's Bush, he'd come to the front door and ask the reason why! But now that she had frightened those little rats of Kelveys and given Kezia a good scolding, her heart felt lighter. That ghastly pressure was gone. She went back to the house humming.

When the Kelveys were well out of sight of Burnells', they sat down to rest on a big red drainpipe by the side of the road. Lil's cheeks were still burning; she took off the hat with the quill and held it on her knee. Dreamily they looked over the hay paddocks, past the creek, to the group of wattles where Logan's cows stood waiting to be milked. What were their thoughts?

Presently our Else nudged up close to her sister. But now she had forgotten the cross lady. She put out a finger and stroked her sister's quill; she smiled her rare smile.

"I seen the little lamp," she said softly.

Then both were silent once more.

Honeymoon

AND WHEN THEY CAME OUT of the lace shop there was their own driver and the cab they called their own cab waiting for them under a plane tree. What luck! Wasn't it luck? Fanny pressed her husband's arm. These things seemed always to be happening to them ever since they — came abroad. Didn't he think so too? But George stood on the pavement edge, lifted his stick, and gave a loud "Hi!" Fanny sometimes felt a little uncomfortable about the way George summoned cabs, but the drivers didn't seem to mind, so it must have been all right. Fat, good-natured, and smiling, they stuffed away the little newspaper they were reading, whipped the cotton cover off the horse, and were ready to obey.

"I say," George said as he helped Fanny in, "suppose we go and have tea at the place where the lobsters grow. Would you like to?"

"Most awfully," said Fanny fervently, as she leaned back wondering why the way George put things made them sound so very nice.

"R-right, *bien.*" He was beside her. "*Allay,*" he cried gaily, and off they went.

Off they went, spanking along lightly, under the green and gold shade of the plane trees, through the small streets that smelled of lemons and fresh coffee, past the fountain square where women, with water-pots lifted, stopped talking to gaze after them, round the corner past the café, with its pink and white umbrellas, green tables, and blue siphons, and so to the sea front. There a wind, light, warm, came flowing over the boundless sea. It touched George, and Fanny it seemed to linger over while they gazed at the dazzling water. And George said, "Jolly, isn't it?" And Fanny, looking dreamy, said, as she said at least twenty times a day since they — came abroad: "Isn't it extraordinary to think that here we are quite alone, away from everybody, with nobody to tell us to go home, or to — to order us about except ourselves?"

George had long since given up answering "Extraordinary!" As a rule he merely kissed her. But now he caught hold of her hand, stuffed it into his pocket, pressed her fingers, and said, "I used to keep a white mouse in my pocket when I was a kid."

"Did you?" said Fanny, who was intensely interested in every-thing George had ever done. "Were you very fond of white mice?"

"Fairly," said George, without conviction. He was looking at something, bobbing out there beyond the bathing steps. Suddenly he almost jumped in his seat. "Fanny!" he cried. "There's a chap out there bathing. Do you see? I'd no idea people had begun. I've been missing it all these days." George glared at the reddened face, the reddened arm, as though he could not look away. "At any rate," he muttered, "wild horses won't keep me from going in tomorrow morning."

Fanny's heart sank. She had heard for years of the frightful dangers of the Mediterranean. It was an absolute death-trap. Beautiful, treacherous Mediterranean. There it lay curled before them, its white, silky paws touching the stones and gone again. . . . But she'd made up her mind long before she was married that never would she be the kind of woman who interfered with her husband's pleasures, so all she said was, airily, "I suppose one has to be very up in the currents, doesn't one?"

"Oh, I don't know," said George. "People talk an awful lot of rot about the danger."

But now they were passing a high wall on the land side, covered with flowering heliotrope, and Fanny's little nose lifted. "Oh, George," she breathed. "The smell! The most divine . . ."

"Topping villa," said George. "Look, you can see it through the palms."

"Isn't it rather large?" said Fanny, who somehow could not look at any villa except as a possible habitation for herself and George.

"Well, you'd need a crowd of people if you stayed there long," replied George. "Deadly, otherwise. I say, it is ripping. I wonder who it belongs to." And he prodded the driver in the back.

The lazy, smiling driver, who had no idea, replied, as he always did on these occasions, that it was the property of a wealthy Spanish family.

"Masses of Spaniards on this coast," commented George, leaning back again, and they were silent until, as they rounded a bend, the big, bone-white hotel-restaurant came into view. Before it there was a small terrace built up against the sea, planted with umbrella palms, set out with tables, and at their approach, from the terrace, from the hotel, waiters came running to receive, to welcome Fanny and George, to cut them off from any possible kind of escape.

"Outside?"

Oh, but of course they would sit outside. The sleek manager, who was marvellously like a fish in a frock-coat, skimmed forward.

"Dis way, sir. Dis way, sir. I have a very nice little table," he gasped. "Just the little table for you, sir, over in de corner. Dis way."

So George, looking most dreadfully bored, and Fanny, trying to look as though she'd spent years of life threading her way through strangers, followed after.

"Here you are, sir. Here you will be very nice," coaxed the manager, taking the vase off the table, and putting it down again as if it were a fresh little bouquet out of the air. But George refused to sit down immediately. He saw through these fellows; he wasn't going to be done. These chaps were always out to rush you. So he put his hands in his pockets, and said to Fanny, very calmly, "This all right for you? Anywhere else you'd prefer? How about over there?" And he nodded to a table right over the other side.

What it was to be a man of the world! Fanny admired him deeply, but all she wanted to do was to sit down and look like everybody else.

"I — I like this," said she.

"Right," said George hastily, and he sat down almost before Fanny, and said quickly, "Tea for two and chocolate éclairs."

"Very good, sir," said the manager, and his mouth opened and shut as though he was ready for another dive under the water. "You will not 'ave toasts to start with? We 'ave very nice toasts, sir."

"No," said George shortly. "You don't want toast, do you, Fanny?"

"Oh no, thank you, George," said Fanny, praying the manager would go.

"Or perhaps de lady might like to look at de live lobsters in de tank while de tea is coming?" And he grimaced and smirked and flicked his serviette like a fin.

George's face grew stony. He said "No" again, and Fanny bent over the table, unbuttoning her gloves. When she looked up the man was gone. George took off his hat, tossed it on to a chair, and pressed back his hair.

"Thank God," said he, "that chap's gone. These foreign fellows bore me stiff. The only way to get rid of them is simply to shut up as you saw I did. Thank heaven!" sighed George again, with so much emotion that if it hadn't been ridiculous Fanny might have imagined that he had been as frightened of the manager as she. As it was she felt a rush of love for George. His hands were on the table, brown, large hands that she knew so well. She longed to take one of them and squeeze it hard. But, to her astonishment, George did just that thing. Leaning across the table, he put his hand over hers, and said, without looking at her, "Fanny, darling Fanny!"

"Oh, George!" It was in that heavenly moment that Fanny heard a *twing-twing-tootle-tootle*, and a light strumming. There's going to be music, she thought, but the music didn't matter just then. Nothing mattered except love. Faintly smiling she gazed into that faintly smiling face, and the feeling was so blissful that she felt inclined to say to George, "Let us stay here — where we are — at this little table. It's perfect, and the sea is perfect. Let us stay." But instead her eyes grew serious.

"Darling," said Fanny. "I want to ask you something fearfully important. Promise me you'll answer. Promise."

"I promise," said George, too solemn to be quite as serious as she.

"It's this." Fanny paused a moment, looked down, looked up again. "Do you feel," she said softly, "that you really know me now? But really, really know *me*?"

It was too much for George. Know his Fanny? He gave a broad, childish grin. "I should jolly well think I do," he said emphatically. "Why, what's up?"

Fanny felt he hadn't quite understood. She went on quickly: "What I mean is this. So often people, even when they love each other, don't seem to — to — it's so hard to say — know each other perfectly. They don't seem to want to. And I think that's awful. They misunderstand each other about the most important things of all." Fanny looked horrified. "George, we couldn't do that, could we? We never could."

"Couldn't be done," laughed George, and he was just going to tell her how much he liked her little nose, when the waiter arrived with the tea and the band struck up. It was a flute, a guitar, and a violin, and it played so gaily that Fanny felt if she wasn't careful even the cups and saucers might grow little wings and fly away. George absorbed three chocolate éclairs, Fanny two. The funny-tasting tea — "Lobster in the kettle," shouted George above the music — was nice all the same, and when the tray was pushed aside and George was smoking, Fanny felt bold enough to look at the other people. But it was the band grouped under one of the dark trees that fascinated her most. The fat man stroking the guitar was like a picture. The dark man playing the flute kept raising his eyebrows as though he was astonished at the sounds that came from it. The fiddler was in shadow.

The music stopped as suddenly as it had begun. It was then she noticed a tall old man with white hair standing beside the musicians. Strange she hadn't noticed him before. He wore a very high, glazed collar, a coat green at the seams, and shamefully shabby button boots. Was he another manager? He did not look like a manager, and yet he stood there gazing over the tables as though thinking of something different and far away from all this. Who could it be?

Presently, as Fanny watched him, he touched the points of his collar with his fingers, coughed slightly, and half turned to the band. It began to play again. Something boisterous, reckless, full of fire, full of passion, was tossed into the air, was tossed to that quiet figure, which clasped its hands, and still with that far-away look, began to sing.

"Good Lord!" said George. It seemed that everybody was equally astonished. Even the little children eating ices stared, with their spoons in the air. . . . Nothing was heard except a thin, faint voice, the memory of a voice singing something in Spanish. It wavered, beat on, touched the high notes, fell again, seemed to implore, to entreat, to beg for something, and then the tune changed, and it was resigned, it bowed down, it knew it was denied.

Almost before the end a little child gave a squeak of laughter, but everybody was smiling — except for Fanny and George. Is life like this too? thought Fanny. There are people like this. There is suffering. And she looked at that gorgeous sea, lapping the land as though it loved it, and the sky, bright with the brightness before evening. Had she and George the right to be so happy? Wasn't it cruel? There must be something else in life which made all these things possible. What was it? She turned to George.

But George had been feeling differently from Fanny. The poor old boy's voice was funny in a way, but, God, how it made you realise what a terrific thing it was to be at the beginning of everything, as they were, he and Fanny! George, too, gazed at the bright, breathing water, and his lips opened as if he could drink it. How fine it was! There was nothing like the sea for making a chap feel fit. And there sat Fanny, his Fanny, leaning forward, breathing so gently.

"Fanny!" George called to her.

As she turned to him something in her soft, wondering look made George feel that for two pins he would jump over the table and carry her off.

"I say," said George rapidly, "let's go, shall we? Let's go back to the hotel. Come. Do, Fanny darling. Let's go now."

The band began to play. "Oh, God!" almost groaned George. "Let's go before the old codger begins squawking again."

And a moment later they were gone.

A Cup of Tea

ROSEMARY FELL was not exactly beautiful. No, you couldn't have called her beautiful. Pretty? Well, if you took her to pieces. . . . But why be so cruel as to take anyone to pieces? She was young, brilliant, extremely modern, exquisitely well dressed, amazingly well read in the newest of the new books, and her parties were the most delicious mixtures of the really important people and . . . artists — quaint creatures, discoveries of hers, some of them too terrifying for words, but others quite presentable and amusing.

Rosemary had been married two years. She had a duck of a boy. No, not Peter — Michael. And her husband absolutely adored her. They were rich, really rich, not just comfortably well off, which is odious and stuffy and sounds like one's grandparents. But if Rosemary wanted to shop she would go to Paris as you and I would go to Bond Street. If she wanted to buy flowers, the car pulled up at that perfect shop in Regent Street, and Rosemary inside the shop just gazed in her dazzled, rather exotic way, and said: "I want those and those and those. Give me four bunches of those. And that jar of roses. Yes, I'll have all the roses in the jar. No, no lilac. I hate lilac. It's got no shape." The attendant bowed and put the lilac out of sight, as though this was only too true; lilac was dreadfully shapeless. "Give me those stumpy little tulips. Those red and white ones." And she was followed to the car by a thin shop-girl staggering under an immense white paper armful that looked like a baby in long clothes. . . .

One winter afternoon she had been buying something in a little antique shop in Curzon Street. It was a shop she liked. For one thing, one usually had it to oneself. And then the man who kept it was ridiculously fond of serving her. He beamed whenever she came in. He clasped his hands; he was so gratified he could scarcely speak. Flattery, of course. All the same, there was something . . .

"You see, madam," he would explain in his low respectful tones, "I love my things. I would rather not part with them than sell them to someone who does not appreciate them, who has not that fine feeling which is so rare. . . ." And, breathing deeply, he unrolled a tiny square of blue velvet and pressed it on the glass counter with his pale finger-tips.

Today it was a little box. He had been keeping it for her. He had shown it to nobody as yet. An exquisite little enamel box with a glaze so fine it looked as though it had been baked in cream. On the lid a minute creature stood under a flowery tree, and a more minute creature still had her arms round his neck. Her hat, really no bigger than a geranium petal, hung from a branch; it had green ribbons. And there was a pink cloud like a watchful cherub floating above their heads. Rosemary took her hands out of her long gloves. She always took off her gloves to examine such things. Yes, she liked it very much. She loved it; it was a great duck. She must have it. And, turning the creamy box, opening and shutting it, she couldn't help noticing how charming her hands were against the blue velvet. The shopman, in some dim cavern of his mind, may have dared to think so too. For he took a pencil, leant over the counter, and his pale bloodless fingers crept timidly towards those rosy, flashing ones, as he murmured gently: "If I may venture to point out to madam, the flowers on the little lady's bodice."

"Charming!" Rosemary admired the flowers. But what was the price? For a moment the shopman did not seem to hear. Then a murmur reached her. "Twenty-eight guineas, madam."

"Twenty-eight guineas." Rosemary gave no sign. She laid the little box down; she buttoned her gloves again. Twenty-eight guineas. Even if one is rich . . . She looked vague. She stared at a plump tea-kettle like a plump hen above the shopman's head, and her voice was dreamy as she answered: "Well, keep it for me — will you? I'll . . ."

But the shopman had already bowed as though keeping it for her was all any human being could ask. He would be willing, of course, to keep it for her for ever.

The discreet door shut with a click. She was outside on the step, gazing at the winter afternoon. Rain was falling, and with the rain it seemed the dark came too, spinning down like ashes. There was a cold bitter taste in the air, and the new-lighted lamps looked sad. Sad were the lights in the houses opposite. Dimly they burned as if regretting something. And people hurried by, hidden under their hateful umbrellas. Rosemary felt a strange pang. She pressed her muff against her breast; she wished she had the little box, too, to cling to. Of course, the car was there. She'd only to cross the pavement. But still she waited. There are moments, horrible moments in life, when one emerges from shelter and looks out, and it's awful. One oughtn't to give way to them. One ought to go home and have an extra-special tea. But at the very instant of thinking that, a young girl, thin, dark, shadowy — where had she come from? — was standing at Rosemary's elbow and a voice like a sigh, almost like a sob, breathed: "Madam, may I speak to you a moment?"

"Speak to me?" Rosemary turned. She saw a little battered creature with enormous eyes, someone quite young, no older than herself, who clutched at her coat-collar with reddened hands, and shivered as though she had just come out of the water.

"M-madam," stammered the voice. "Would you let me have the price of a cup of tea?"

"A cup of tea?" There was something simple, sincere in that voice; it wasn't in the least the voice of a beggar. "Then have you no money at all?" asked Rosemary.

"None, madam," came the answer.

"How extraordinary!" Rosemary peered through the dusk, and the girl gazed back at her. How more than extraordinary! And suddenly it seemed to Roisemary such an adventure. It was like something out of a novel by Dostoevsky, this meeting in the dusk. Supposing she took the girl home? Supposing she did do one of those things she was always reading about or seeing on the stage, what would happen? It would be thrilling. And she heard herself saying afterwards to the amazement of her friends: "I simply took her home with me," as she stepped forward and said to that dim person beside her: "Come home to tea with me."

The girl drew back startled. She even stopped shivering for a moment. Rosemary put out a hand and touched her arm. "I mean it," she said, smiling. And she felt how simple and kind her smile was. "Why won't you? Do. Come home with me now in my car and have tea."

"You — you don't mean it, madam," said the girl, and there was pain in her voice.

"But I do," cried Rosemary. "I want you to. To please me. Come along."

The girl put her fingers to her lips and her eyes devoured Rosemary. "You're — you're not taking me to the police station?" she stammered.

"The police station!" Rosemary laughed out. "Why should I be so cruel? No, I only want to make you warm and to hear — anything you care to tell me."

Hungry people are easily led. The footman held the door of the car open, and a moment later they were skimming through the dusk.

"There!" said Rosemary. She had a feeling of triumph as she slipped her hand through the velvet strap. She could have said, "Now I've got you," as she gazed at the little captive she had netted. But of course she meant it kindly. Oh, more than kindly. She was going to prove to this girl that — wonderful things did happen in life, that — fairy godmothers were real, that — rich people had hearts, and that women *were* sisters. She turned impulsively, saying: "Don't be frightened. After all, why shouldn't you come back with me? We're both women. If I'm the more fortunate, you ought to expect . . ."

But happily at that moment, for she didn't know how the sentence was going to end, the car stopped. The bell was rung, the door opened, and with a charming, protecting, almost embracing movement, Rosemary drew the other into the hall. Warmth, softness, light, a sweet scent, all those things so familiar to her she never even thought about them, she watched that other receive. It was fascinating. She was like the rich little girl in her nursery with all the cupboards to open, all the boxes to unpack.

"Come, come upstairs," said Rosemary, longing to begin to be generous. "Come up to my room." And, besides, she wanted to spare this poor little thing from being stared at by the servants; she decided as they mounted the stairs she would not even ring for Jeanne, but take off her things by herself. The great thing was to be natural!

And "There!" cried Rosemary again, as they reached her beautiful big bedroom with the curtains drawn, the fire leaping on her wonderful lacquer furniture, her gold cushions and the primrose and blue rugs.

The girl stood just inside the door; she seemed dazed. But Rosemary didn't mind that.

"Come and sit down," she cried, dragging her big chair up to the fire, "in this comfy chair. Come and get warm. You look so dreadfully cold."

"I daren't, madam," said the girl, and she edged backwards.

"Oh, please," — Rosemary ran forward — "you mustn't be frightened, you mustn't, really. Sit down, and when I've taken off my things we shall go into the next room and have tea and be cosy. Why are you afraid?" And gently she half pushed the thin figure into its deep cradle.

But there was no answer. The girl stayed just as she had been put, with her hands by her sides and her mouth slightly open. To be quite sincere, she looked rather stupid. But Rosemary wouldn't acknowledge it. She leant over her, saying: "Won't you take off your hat? Your pretty hair is all wet. And one is so much more comfortable without a hat, isn't one?"

There was a whisper that sounded like "Very good, madam," and the crushed hat was taken off.

"And let me help you off with your coat, too," said Rosemary.

The girl stood up. But she held on to the chair with one hand and let Rosemary pull. It was quite an effort. The other scarcely helped her at all. She seemed to stagger like a child, and the thought came and went through Rosemary's mind, that if people wanted helping they must respond a little, just a little, otherwise it became very difficult indeed. And what was she to do with the coat now? She left it on the floor, and the hat too. She was just going to take a cigarette off the mantelpiece when the girl said quickly, but so lightly and strangely: "I'm very sorry, madam, but I'm going to faint. I shall go off, madam, if I don't have something."

"Good heavens, how thoughtless I am!" Rosemary rushed to the bell.

"Tea! Tea at once! And some brandy immediately!"

The maid was gone again, but the girl almost cried out: "No, I don't want no brandy. I never drink brandy. It's a cup of tea I want, madam." And she burst into tears.

It was a terrible and fascinating moment. Rosemary knelt beside her chair.

"Don't cry, poor little thing," she said. "Don't cry." And she gave the other her lace handkerchief. She really was touched beyond words. She put her arm round those thin, bird-like shoulders.

Now at last the other forgot to be shy, forgot everything except that they were both women, and gasped out: "I can't go on no longer like this. I can't bear it. I can't bear it. I shall do away with myself. I can't bear no more."

"You shan't have to. I'll look after you. Don't cry any more. Don't you see what a good thing it was that you met me? We'll have tea and you'll tell me everything. And I shall arrange something. I promise. *Do* stop crying. It's so exhausting. Please!"

The other did stop just in time for Rosemary to get up before the tea came. She had the table placed between them. She plied the poor little creature with everything, all the sandwiches, all the bread and butter, and every time her cup was empty she filled it with tea, cream and sugar. People always said sugar was so nourishing. As for herself she didn't eat; she smoked and looked away tactfully so that the other should not be shy.

And really the effect of that slight meal was marvellous. When the tea-table was carried away a new being, a light, frail creature with tangled hair, dark lips, deep, lighted eyes, lay back in the big chair in a kind of sweet languor, looking at the blaze. Rosemary lit a fresh cigarette; it was time to begin.

"And when did you have your last meal?" she asked softly.

But at that moment the door-handle turned.

"Rosemary, may I come in?" It was Philip.

"Of course."

He came in. "Oh, I'm so sorry," he said, and stopped and stared.

"It's quite all right," said Rosemary, smiling. "This is my friend, Miss —"

"Smith, madam," said the languid figure, who was strangely still and unafraid.

"Smith," said Rosemary. "We are going to have a little talk."

"Oh yes," said Philip. "Quite," and his eye caught sight of the coat and hat on the floor. He came over to the fire and turned his back on it. "It's a beastly afternoon," he said curiously, still looking at that listless figure, looking at its hands and boots, and then at Rosemary again.

"Yes, isn't it?" said Rosemary enthusiastically. "Vile."

Philip smiled his charming smile. "As a matter of fact," said he, "I wanted you to come into the library for a moment. Would you? Will Miss Smith excuse us?"

The big eyes were raised to him, but Rosemary answered for her: "Of course she will." And they went out of the room together.

"I say," said Philip, when they were alone. "Explain. Who is she? What does it all mean?"

Rosemary, laughing, leaned against the door and said: "I picked her up in Curzon Street. Really. She's a real pick-up. She asked me for the price of a cup of tea, and I brought her home with me."

"But what on earth are you going to do with her?" cried Philip.

"Be nice to her," said Rosemary quickly. "Be frightfully nice to her. Look after her. I don't know how. We haven't talked yet. But show her — treat her — make her feel —"

"My darling girl," said Philip, "you're quite mad, you know. It simply can't be done."

"I knew you'd say that," retorted Rosemary. "Why not? I want to. Isn't that a reason? And besides, one's always reading about these things. I decided — "

"But," said Philip slowly, and he cut the end of a cigar, "she's so astonishingly pretty."

"Pretty?" Rosemary was so surprised that she blushed. "Do you think so? I — I hadn't thought about it."

"Good Lord!" Philip struck a match. "She's absolutely lovely. Look again, my child. However . . . I think you're making a ghastly mistake. Sorry, darling, if I'm crude and all that. But let me know if Miss Smith is going to dine with us in time for me to look up *The Milliner's Gazette.*"

"You absurd creature!" said Rosemary, and she went out of the library, but not back to her bedroom. She went to her writing-room and sat down at her desk. Pretty! Absolutely lovely! Bowled over! Her heart beat like a heavy bell. Pretty! Lovely! She drew her cheque-book towards her. But no, cheques would be no use, of course. She opened a drawer and took out five pound notes, looked at them, put two back, and holding the three squeezed in her hand, she went back to her bedroom.

Half an hour later Philip was still in the library, when Rosemary came in.

"I only wanted to tell you," said she, and she leaned against the door again and looked at him with her dazzled exotic gaze, "Miss Smith won't dine with us tonight."

Philip put down the paper. "Oh, what's happened? Previous engagement?"

Rosemary came over and sat down on his knee. "She insisted on going," said she, "so I gave the poor little thing a present of money, I couldn't keep her against her will, could I?" she added softly.

Rosemary had just done her hair, darkened her eyes a little, and put on her pearls. She put up her hands and touched Philip's cheeks.

"Do you like me?" said she, and her tone, sweet, husky, troubled him.

"I like you awfully," he said, and he held her tighter. "Kiss me." There was a pause.

Then Rosemary said dreamily: "I saw a fascinating little box today. It cost twenty-eight guineas. May I have it?"

Philip jumped her on his knee. "You may, little wasteful one," said he.

But that was not really what Rosemary wanted to say.

"Philip," she whispered, and she pressed his head against her bosom, "am I *pretty*?"

Taking the Veil

IT SEEMED IMPOSSIBLE that anyone should be unhappy on such a beautiful morning. Nobody was, decided Edna, except herself. The windows were flung wide in the houses. From within there came the sound of pianos, little hands chased after each other and ran away from each other, practising scales. The trees fluttered in the sunny gardens, all bright with spring flowers. Street boys whistled, a little dog barked; people passed by, walking so lightly, so swiftly, they looked as though they wanted to break into a run. Now she actually saw in the distance a parasol, peach-coloured, the first parasol of the year.

Perhaps even Edna did not look quite as unhappy as she felt. It is not easy to look tragic at eighteen, when you are extremely pretty, with the cheeks and lips and shining eyes of perfect health. Above all, when you are wearing a French blue frock and your new spring hat trimmed with cornflowers. True, she carried under her arm a book bound in horrid black leather. Perhaps the book provided a gloomy note, but only by accident; it was the ordinary Library binding. For Edna had made going to the Library an excuse for getting out of the house to think, to realise what had happened, to decide somehow what was to be done now.

An awful thing had happened. Quite suddenly, at the theatre last night, when she and Jimmy were seated side by side in the dress-circle, without a moment's warning — in fact, she had just finished a chocolate almond and passed the box to him again — she had fallen in love with an actor. But — fallen — in — love. . . .

The feeling was unlike anything she had ever imagined before. It wasn't in the least pleasant. It was hardly thrilling. Unless you can call the most dreadful sensation of hopeless misery, despair, agony and wretchedness, thrilling. Combined with the certainty that if that actor met her on the pavement after, while Jimmy was fetching their cab, she would follow him to the ends of the earth, at a nod, at a sign, without giving another thought to Jimmy or her father and mother or her happy home and countless friends again. . . .

The play had begun fairly cheerfully. That was at the chocolate almond stage. Then the hero had gone blind. Terrible moment! Edna had cried so much she had to borrow Jimmy's folded, smooth-feeling handkerchief as well. Not that crying mattered. Whole rows were in tears. Even the men blew their noses with a loud trumpeting noise and tried to peer at the programme instead of looking at the stage. Jimmy, most mercifully dry-eyed — for what would she have done without his handkerchief? — squeezed her free hand, and whispered "Cheer up, darling girl!" And it was then she had taken a last chocolate almond to please him and passed the box again. Then there had been that ghastly scene with the hero alone on the stage in a deserted room at twilight, with a band playing outside and the sound of cheering coming from the street. He had tried — ah! how painfully, how pitifully! — to grope his way to the window. He had succeeded at last. There he stood holding the curtain while one beam of light, just one beam, shone full on his raised sightless face, and the band faded away into the distance. . . .

It was — really, it was absolutely — oh, the most — it was simply — in fact, from that moment Edna knew that life could never be the same. She drew her hand away from Jimmy's, leaned back, and shut the chocolate box for ever. This at last was love!

Edna and Jimmy were engaged. She had had her hair up for a year and a half; they had been publicly engaged for a year. But they had known they were going to marry each other ever since they walked in the Botanical Gardens with their nurses, and sat on the grass with a wine biscuit and a piece of barley-sugar each for their tea. It was so much an accepted thing that Edna had worn a wonderfully good imitation of an engagement-ring out of a cracker all the time she was at school. And up till now they had been devoted to each other.

But now it was over. It was so completely over that Edna found it difficult to believe that Jimmy did not realise it too. She smiled wisely, sadly, as she turned into the gardens of the Convent of the Sacred Heart and mounted the path that led through them to Hill Street. How much better to know it now than to wait until after they were married! Now it was possible that Jimmy would get over it. No, it was no use deceiving herself; he would never get over it! His life was wrecked, was ruined; that was inevitable. But he was young. . . . Time, people always said, Time might make a little, just a little difference. In forty years when he was an old man, he might be able to think of her calmly — perhaps. But she — what did the future hold for her?

Edna had reached the top of the path. There under a new-leafed tree, hung with little bunches of white flowers, she sat down on a green bench and looked over the Convent flower-beds. In the one nearest to her there grew tender stocks, with a border of blue, shell-like pansies, with at one corner a clump of creamy freesias, their light spears of green criss-crossed over the flowers. The Convent pigeons were tumbling high in the air, and she could hear the voice of Sister Agnes who was giving a singing lesson. *Ah-me*, sounded the deep tones of the nun, and *Ah-me*, they were echoed. . . .

If she did not marry Jimmy, of course she would marry nobody. The man she was in love with, the famous actor — Edna had far too much common-sense not to realise that would never be. It was very odd. She didn't even want it to be. Her love was too intense for that. It had to be endured, silently; it had to torment her. It was, she supposed, simply that kind of love.

"But Edna!" cried Jimmy. "Can you never change? Can I never hope again?"

Oh, what sorrow to have to say it, but it must be said. "No, Jimmy, I will never change."

Edna bowed her head; and a little flower fell on her lap, and the voice of Sister Agnes cried suddenly *Ah-no*, and the echo came, *Ah-no*. . . .

At that moment the future was revealed. Edna saw it all. She was astonished; it took her breath away at first. But, after all, what could be more natural? She would go into a convent. . . . Her father and mother do everything to dissuade her, in vain. As for Jimmy, his state of mind hardly bears thinking about. Why can't they understand? How can they add to her suffering like this? The world is cruel, terribly cruel! After a last scene when she gives away her jewellery and so on to her best friends — she so calm, they so broken-hearted — into a convent she goes. No, one moment. The very evening of her going is the actor's last evening at Port Willin. He receives by a strange messenger a box. It is full of white flowers. But there is no name, no card. Nothing? Yes, under the roses, wrapped in a white handkerchief, Edna's last photograph with, written underneath,

The world forgetting, by the world forgot.

Edna sat very still under the trees; she clasped the black book in her fingers as though it were her missal. She takes the name of Sister Angela. Snip! Snip! All her lovely hair is cut off. Will she be allowed to send one curl to Jimmy? It is contrived somehow.

And in a blue gown with a white head-band Sister Angela goes from the convent to the chapel, from the chapel to the convent with something unearthly in her look, in her sorrowful eyes, and in the gentle smile with which they greet the little children who run to her. A saint! She hears it whispered as she paces the chill, wax-smelling corridors. A saint! And visitors to the chapel are told of the nun whose voice is heard above the other voices, of her youth, her beauty, of her tragic, tragic love. "There is a man in this town whose life is ruined. . . ."

A big bee, a golden furry fellow, crept into a freesia, and the delicate flower leaned over, swung, shook; and when the bee flew away it fluttered still as though it were laughing. Happy, careless flower!

Sister Angela looked at it and said, "Now it is winter." One night, lying in her icy cell, she hears a cry. Some stray animal is out there in the garden, a kitten or a lamb, or — well, whatever little animal might be there. Up rises the sleepless nun. All in white, shivering but fearless, she goes and brings it in. But next morning, when the bell rings for matins, she is found tossing in high fever . . . in delirium . . . and she never recovers. In three days all is over. The service has been said in the chapel, and she is buried in the corner of the cemetery reserved for the nuns, where there are plain little crosses of wood. Rest in Peace, Sister Angela. . . .

Now it is evening. Two old people leaning on each other come slowly to the grave and kneel down sobbing, "Our daughter! Our only daughter!" Now there comes another. He is all in black; he comes slowly. But when he is there and lifts his black hat, Edna sees to her horror his hair is snow-white. Jimmy! Too late, too late! The tears are running down his face; he is crying *now*. Too late, too late! The wind shakes the leafless trees in the churchyard. He gives one awful bitter cry.

Edna's black book fell with a thud on the garden path. She jumped up, her heart beating. My darling! No, it's not too late. It's all been a mistake, a terrible dream. Oh, that white hair! How could she have done it? She has not done it. Oh, heavens! Oh, what happiness! She is free, young, and nobody knows her secret. Everything is still possible for her and Jimmy. The house they have planned may still be built, the little solemn boy with his hands behind his back watching them plant the standard roses may still be born. His baby sister . . . But when Edna got as far as his baby sister, she stretched out her arms as though the little love came flying through the air to her, and gazing at the garden, at the white sprays on the tree, at those darling pigeons blue against the blue, and the Convent with its narrow windows, she realised that now at last for the first time in her life — she had never imagined any feeling like it before — she knew what it was to be in love, but — in — love!

The Fly

"Y'ARE VERY SNUG IN HERE," piped old Mr Woodifield, and he peered out of the great, green-leather armchair by his friend the boss's desk as a baby peers out of its pram. His talk was over; it was time for him to be off. But he did not want to go. Since he had retired, since his . . . stroke, the wife and the girls kept him boxed up in the house every day of the week except Tuesday. On Tuesday he was dressed and brushed and allowed to cut back to the City for the day. Though what he did there the wife and girls couldn't imagine. Made a nuisance of himself to his friends, they supposed. . . . Well, perhaps so. All the same, we cling to our last pleasures as the tree clings to its last leaves. So there sat old Woodifield, smoking a cigar and staring almost greedily at the boss, who rolled in his office chair, stout, rosy, five years older than he, and still going strong, still at the helm. It did one good to see him.

Wistfully, admiringly, the old voice added, "It's snug in here, upon my word!"

"Yes, it's comfortable enough," agreed the boss, and he flipped the *Financial Times* with a paper-knife. As a matter of fact he was proud of his room; he liked to have it admired, especially by old Woodifield. It gave him a feeling of deep, solid satisfaction to be planted there in the midst of it in full view of that frail old figure in the muffler.

"I've had it done up lately," he explained, as he had explained for the past — how many? — weeks. "New carpet," and he pointed to the bright red carpet with a pattern of large white rings. "New furniture," and he nodded towards the massive bookcase and the table with legs like twisted treacle. "Electric heating!" He waved almost exultantly towards the five transparent, pearly sausages glowing so softly in the tilted copper pan.

But he did not draw old Woodifield's attention to the photograph over the table of a grave-looking boy in uniform standing in one of those spectral photographers' parks with photographers' storm-clouds behind him. It was not new. It had been there for over six years.

"There was something I wanted to tell you," said old Woodifield, and his eyes grew dim remembering. "Now what was it? I had it in my mind when I started out this morning." His hands began to tremble, and patches of red showed above his beard.

Poor old chap, he's on his last pins, thought the boss. And, feeling kindly, he winked at the old man, and said jokingly, "I tell you what. I've got a little drop of something here that'll do you good before you go out into the cold again. It's beautiful stuff. It wouldn't hurt a child." He took a key off his watch-chain, unlocked a cupboard below his desk, and drew forth a dark, squat bottle. "That's the medicine," said he. "And the man from whom I got it told me on the strict Q.T. it came from the cellars at Windsor Castle."

Old Woodifield's mouth fell open at the sight. He couldn't have looked more surprised if the boss had produced a rabbit.

"It's whisky, ain't it?" he piped feebly.

The boss turned the bottle and lovingly showed him the label. Whisky it was.

"D'you know," said he, peering up at the boss wonderingly, "they won't let me touch it at home." And he looked as though he was going to cry.

"Ah, that's where we know a bit more than the ladies," cried the boss, swooping across for two tumblers that stood on the table with the water-bottle, and pouring a generous finger into each. "Drink it down. It'll do you good. And don't put any water with it. It's sacrilege to tamper with stuff like this. Ah!" He tossed off his, pulled out his handkerchief, hastily wiped his moustaches, and cocked an eye at old Woodifield, who was rolling his in his chaps.

The old man swallowed, was silent a moment, and then said faintly, "It's nutty!"

But it warmed him; it crept into his chill old brain — he remembered.

"That was it," he said, heaving himself out of his chair. "I thought you'd like to know. The girls were in Belgium last week having a look at poor Reggie's grave, and they happened to come across your boy's. They're quite near each other, it seems."

Old Woodifield paused, but the boss made no reply. Only a quiver in his eyelids showed that he heard.

"The girls were delighted with the way the place is kept," piped the old voice. "Beautifully looked after. Couldn't be better if they were at home. You've not been across, have yer?"

"No, no!" For various reasons the boss had not been across.

"There's miles of it," quavered old Woodifield, "and it's all as neat as a garden. Flowers growing on all the graves. Nice broad paths." It was plain from his voice how much he liked a nice broad path.

The pause came again. Then the old man brightened wonderfully.

"D'you know what the hotel made the girls pay for a pot of jam?" he piped. "Ten francs! Robbery, I call it. It was a little pot, so Gertrude says, no bigger than a half-crown. And she hadn't taken more than a spoonful when they charged her ten francs. Gertrude brought the pot away with her to teach 'em a lesson. Quite right, too; it's trading on our feelings. They think because we're over there having a look round we're ready to pay anything. That's what it is." And he turned towards the door.

"Quite right, quite right!" cried the boss, though what was quite right he hadn't the least idea. He came round by his desk, followed the shuffling footsteps to the door, and saw the old fellow out. Woodifield was gone.

For a long moment the boss stayed, staring at nothing, while the grey-haired office messenger, watching him, dodged in and out of his cubby-hole like a dog that expects to be taken for a run. Then: "I'll see nobody for half an hour, Macey," said the boss. "Understand? Nobody at all."

"Very good, sir."

The door shut, the firm heavy steps recrossed the bright carpet, the fat body plumped down in the spring chair, and leaning forward, the boss covered his face with his hands. He wanted, he intended, he had arranged to weep. . . .

It had been a terrible shock to him when old Woodifield sprang that remark upon him about the boy's grave. It was exactly as though the earth had opened and he had seen the boy lying there with Woodifield's girls staring down at him. For it was strange. Although over six years had passed away, the boss never thought of the boy except as lying unchanged, unblemished in his uniform, asleep for ever. "My son!" groaned the boss. But no tears came yet. In the past, in the first months and even years after the boy's death, he had only to say those words to be overcome by such grief that nothing short of a violent fit of weeping could relieve him. Time, he had declared then, he had told everybody, could make no difference. Other men perhaps might recover, might live their loss down, but not he. How was it possible? His boy was an only son. Ever since his birth the boss had worked at building up this business for him; it had no other meaning if it was not for the boy. Life itself had come to have no other meaning. How on earth could he have slaved, denied himself, kept going all those years without the promise for ever before him of the boy's stepping into his shoes and carrying on where he left off?

And that promise had been so near being fulfilled. The boy had been in the office learning the ropes for a year before the war. Every morning they had started off together; they had come back by the same train. And what congratulations he had received as the boy's father! No wonder; he had taken to it marvellously. As to his popularity with the staff, every man jack of them down to old Macey couldn't make enough of the boy. And he wasn't in the least spoilt. No, he was just his bright natural self, with the right word for everybody, with that boyish look and his habit of saying, "Simply splendid!"

But that was all over and done with as though it never had been. The day had come when Macey had handed him the telegram that brought the whole place crashing about his head. "Deeply regret to inform you . . ." And he had left the office a broken man, with his life in ruins.

Six years ago, six years. . . . How quickly time passed! It might have happened yesterday. The boss took his hands from his face; he was puzzled. Something seemed to be wrong with him. He wasn't feeling as he wanted to feel. He decided to get up and have a look at the boy's photograph. But it wasn't a favourite photograph of his; the expression was unnatural. It was cold, even stern-looking. The boy had never looked like that.

At that moment the boss noticed that a fly had fallen into his broad inkpot, and was trying feebly but desperately to clamber out again. Help! help! said those struggling legs. But the sides of the inkpot were wet and slippery; it fell back again and began to swim. The boss took up a pen, picked the fly out of the ink, and shook it on to a piece of blotting-paper. For a fraction of a second it lay still on the dark patch that oozed round it. Then the front legs waved, took hold, and, pulling its small, sodden body up, it began the immense task of cleaning the ink from its wings. Over and under, over and under, went a leg along a wing as the stone goes over and under the scythe. Then there was a pause, while the fly, seeming to stand on the tips of its toes, tried to expand first one wing and then the other. It succeeded at last, and, sitting down, it began, like a minute cat, to clean its face. Now one could imagine that the little front legs rubbed against each other lightly, joyfully. The horrible danger was over; it had escaped; it was ready for life again.

But just then the boss had an idea. He plunged his pen back into the ink, leaned his thick wrist on the blotting-paper, and as the fly tried its wings down came a great heavy blot. What would it make of that? What indeed! The little beggar seemed absolutely cowed, stunned, and afraid to move because of what would happen next. But then, as if painfully, it dragged itself forward. The front legs waved, caught hold, and, more slowly this time, the task began from the beginning.

He's a plucky little devil, thought the boss, and he felt a real admiration for the fly's courage. That was the way to tackle things; that was the right spirit. Never say die; it was only a question of . . . But the fly had again finished its laborious task, and the boss had just time to refill his pen, to shake fair and square on the new-cleaned body yet another dark drop. What about it this time? A painful moment of suspense followed. But behold, the front legs were again waving; the boss felt a rush of relief. He leaned over the fly and said to it tenderly, "You artful little b . . ." And he actually had the brilliant notion of breathing on it to help the drying process. All the same, there was something timid and weak about its efforts now, and the boss decided that this time should be the last, as he dipped the pen deep into the inkpot.

It was. The last blot fell on the soaked blotting-paper, and the draggled fly lay in it and did not stir. The back legs were stuck to the body; the front legs were not to be seen.

"Come on," said the boss. "Look sharp!" And he stirred it with his pen — in vain. Nothing happened or was likely to happen. The fly was dead.

The boss lifted the corpse on the end of the paper-knife and flung it into the waste-paper basket. But such a grinding feeling of wretchedness seized him that he felt positively frightened. He started forward and pressed the bell for Macey.

"Bring me some fresh blotting-paper," he said sternly, "and look sharp about it." And while the old dog padded away he fell to wondering what it was he had been thinking about before. What was it? It was . . . He took out his handkerchief and passed it inside his collar. For the life of him he could not remember.

The Canary

YOU SEE THAT BIG NAIL to the right of the front door? I
• • • can scarcely look at it even now and yet I could not bear
to take it out. I should like to think it was there always even after
my time. I sometimes hear the next people saying, "There must
have been a cage hanging from there." And it comforts me; I feel
he is not quite forgotten.

. . . You cannot imagine how wonderfully he sang. It was not like
the singing of other canaries. And that isn't just my fancy. Often,
from the window, I used to see people stop at the gate to listen,
or they would lean over the fence by the mock-orange for quite a
long time — carried away. I suppose it sounds absurd to you — it
wouldn't if you had heard him — but it really seemed to me that
he sang whole songs with a beginning and an end to them.

For instance, when I'd finished the house in the afternoon, and
changed my blouse and brought my sewing on to the veranda
here, he used to hop, hop, hop from one perch to another, tap
against the bars as if to attract my attention, sip a little water just
as a professional singer might, and then break into a song so exquisite that I had to put my needle down to listen to him. I can't
describe it; I wish I could. But it was always the same, every afternoon, and I felt that I understood every note of it.

. . . I loved him. How I loved him! Perhaps it does not matter
so very much what it is one loves in this world. But love something
one must. Of course there was always my little house and the
garden, but for some reason they were never enough. Flowers
respond wonderfully, but they don't sympathise. Then I loved the
evening star. Does that sound foolish? I used to go into the back-
yard, after sunset, and wait for it until it shone above the dark gum
tree. I used to whisper, "There you are, my darling." And just in
that first moment it seemed to be shining for me alone. It seemed
to understand this . . . something which is like longing, and yet
it is not longing. Or regret — it is more like regret. And yet regret
for what? I have much to be thankful for.

. . . But after he came into my life I forgot the evening star; I did not need it any more. But it was strange. When the Chinaman who came to the door with birds to sell held him up in his tiny cage, and instead of fluttering, fluttering, like the poor little gold-finches, he gave a faint, small chirp, I found myself saying, just as I had said to the star over the gum tree, "There you are, my darling." From that moment he was mine.

. . . It surprises me even now to remember how he and I shared each other's lives. The moment I came down in the morning and took the cloth off his cage he greeted me with a drowsy little note. I knew it meant "Missus! Missus!" Then I hung him on the nail outside while I got my three young men their breakfasts, and I never brought him in until we had the house to ourselves again. Then, when the washing-up was done, it was quite a little enter-tainment. I spread a newspaper over a corner of the table, and when I put the cage on it he used to beat with his wings despair-ingly, as if he didn't know what was coming. "You're a regular little actor," I used to scold him. I scraped the tray, dusted it with fresh sand, filled his seed and water bins, tucked a piece of chickweed and half a chilli between the bars. And I am perfectly certain he understood and appreciated every item of this little performance. You see by nature he was exquisitely neat. There was never a speck on his perch. And you'd only to see him enjoy his bath to realise he had a real small passion for cleanliness. His bath was put in last. And the moment it was in he positively leapt into it. First he flut-tered one wing, then the other, then he ducked his head and dabbled his breast feathers. Drops of water were scattered all over the kitchen, but still he would not get out. I used to say to him, "Now that's quite enough. You're only showing off." And at last out he hopped and, standing on one leg, he began to peck himself dry. Finally he gave a shake, a flick, a twitter and he lifted his throat — Oh, I can hardly bear to recall it. I was always cleaning the knives at the time. And it almost seemed to me the knives sang too, as I rubbed them bright on the board.

. . . Company, you see — that was what he was. Perfect com-pany. If you have lived alone you will realise how precious that is. Of course there were my three young men who came in to supper every evening, and sometimes they stayed in the dining-room afterwards reading the paper. But I could not expect them to be interested in the little things that made my day. Why should they be? I was nothing to them. In fact, I overheard them one evening talking about me on the stairs as "the Scarecrow". No matter. It doesn't matter. Not in the least. I quite understand. They are young. Why should I mind? But I remember feeling so especially thankful that I was not quite alone that evening. I told him, after they had gone out. I said, "Do you know what they call Missus?" And he put his head on one side and looked at me with his little bright eye until I could not help laughing. It seemed to amuse him.

. . . Have you kept birds? If you haven't all this must sound, perhaps, exaggerated. People have the idea that birds are heartless, cold little creatures, not like dogs or cats. My washerwoman used to say on Mondays when she wondered why I didn't keep "a nice fox-terrier", "There's no comfort, Miss, in a canary." Untrue. Dreadfully untrue. I remember one night. I had had a very awful dream — dreams can be dreadfully cruel — even after I had woken up I could not get over it. So I put on my dressing-gown and went down to the kitchen for a glass of water. It was a winter night and raining hard. I suppose I was still half asleep, but through the kitchen window, that hadn't a blind, it seemed to me the dark was staring in, spying. And suddenly I felt it was unbearable that I had no one to whom I could say "I've had such a dreadful dream," or — "Hide me from the dark." I even covered my face for a minute. And then there came a little "Sweet! Sweet!" His cage was on the table, and the cloth had slipped so that a chink of light shone through. "Sweet! Sweet!" said the darling little fellow again, softly, as much as to say, "I'm here, Missus! I'm here!" That was so beautifully comforting that I nearly cried.

. . . And now he's gone. I shall never have another bird, another pet of any kind. How could I? When I found him, lying on his back, with his eye dim and his claws wrung, when I realised that never again should I hear my darling sing, something seemed to die in me. My heart felt hollow, as if it was his cage. I shall get over it. Of course. I must. One can get over anything in time. And people always say I have a cheerful disposition. They are quite right. I thank my God I have.

. . . All the same, without being morbid, and giving way to — to memories and so on, I must confess that there does seem to me something sad in life. It is hard to say what it is. I don't mean the sorrow that we all know, like illness and poverty and death. No, it is something different. It is there, deep down, deep down, part of one, like one's breathing. However hard I work and tire myself

I have only to stop to know it is there, waiting. I often wonder if everybody feels the same. One can never know. But isn't it extraordinary that under his sweet, joyful little singing it was just this — sadness? — Ah, what is it? — that I heard.

A Married Man's Story

IT IS EVENING. Supper is over. We have left the small, cold dining-room, we have come back to the sitting-room where there is a fire. All is as usual. I am sitting at my writing-table which is placed across a corner so that I am behind it, as it were, and facing the room. The lamp with the green shade is alight; I have before me two large books of reference, both open, a pile of papers. . . . All the paraphernalia, in fact, of an extremely occupied man. My wife, with her little boy on her lap, is in a low chair before the fire. She is about to put him to bed before she clears away the dishes and piles them up in the kitchen for the servant girl tomorrow morning. But the warmth, the quiet, and the sleepy baby, have made her dreamy. One of his red woollen boots is off, one is on. She sits, bent forward, clasping the little bare foot, staring into the glow, and as the fire quickens, falls, flares again, her shadow — an immense *Mother and Child* — is here and gone again upon the wall. . . .

Outside it is raining. I like to think of that cold drenched window behind the blind, and beyond, the dark bushes in the garden, their broad leaves bright with rain, and beyond the fence, the gleaming road with the two hoarse little gutters singing against each other, and the wavering reflections of the lamps, like fishes' tails. While I am here, I am there, lifting my face to the dim sky, and it seems to me it must be raining all over the world — that the whole earth is drenched, is sounding with a soft, quick patter or hard, steady drumming, or gurgling and something that is like sobbing and laughing mingled together, and that light, playful splashing that is of water falling into still lakes and flowing rivers. And all at one and the same moment I am arriving in a strange city, slipping under the hood of the cab while the driver whips the cover off the breathing horse, running from shelter to shelter, dodging someone, swerving by someone else. I am conscious of tall houses, their doors and shutters sealed against the night, of dripping balconies and sodden flower-pots. I am brushing through deserted gardens and falling into moist smelling summer-houses (you know how soft and almost crumbling the wood of a summer-house is in the rain); I am standing on the dark quayside giving my ticket into the wet, red hand of the old sailor in an oilskin. How strong the sea smells! How loudly the tied-up boats knock against one another! I am crossing the wet stackyard, hooded in an old sack, carrying a lantern, while the house-dog, like a soaking doormat, springs, shakes himself over me. And now I am walking along a deserted road — it is impossible to miss the puddles, and the trees are stirring — stirring.

But one could go on with such a catalogue for ever — on and on — until one lifted the single arum lily leaf and discovered the tiny snails clinging, until one counted . . . and what then? Aren't those just the signs, the traces of my feeling? The bright green streaks made by someone who walks over the dewy grass? Not the feeling itself. And as I think that a mournful, glorious voice begins to sing in my bosom. Yes, perhaps that is nearer what I mean. What a voice! What power! What velvety softness! Marvellous!

Suddenly my wife turns round quickly. She knows — how long has she known? — that I am not "working". It is strange that with her full, open gaze she should smile so timidly — and that she should say in such a hestitating voice, "What are you thinking?"

I smile and draw two fingers across my forehead in the way I have. "Nothing," I answer softly.

At that she stirs and, still trying not to make it sound important, she says, "Oh, but you must have been thinking of something!"

Then I really meet her gaze, meet it fully, and I fancy her face quivers. Will she never grow accustomed to these simple — one might say — everyday little lies? Will she never learn not to expose herself — or to build up defences?

"Truly, I was thinking of nothing."

There! I seem to see it dart at her. She turns away, pulls the other red sock off the baby, sits him up, and begins to unbutton him behind. I wonder if that little soft rolling bundle sees anything, feels anything? Now she turns him over on her knee, and in this light, his soft arms and legs waving, he is extraordinarily like a young crab. A queer thing is I can't connect him with my wife and myself — I've never accepted him as ours. Each time when I come into the hall and see the perambulator I catch myself thinking: "H'm, someone has brought a baby!" Or, when his crying wakes me at night, I feel inclined to blame my wife for having brought the baby in from outside. The truth is, that though one might sus-

pect her of strong maternal feelings, my wife doesn't seem to me
the type of woman who bears children in her own body. There's
an immense difference! Where is that . . . animal ease and playfulness, that quick kissing and cuddling one has been taught to
expect of young mothers? She hadn't a sign of it. I believe that
when she ties its bonnet she feels like an aunt and not a mother.
But of course I may be wrong; she may be passionately devoted.
. . . I don't think so. At any rate, isn't it a trifle indecent to feel
like this about one's own wife? Indecent or not, one has these
feelings. And one other thing. How can I reasonably expect my
wife, *a broken-hearted woman*, to spend her time tossing the baby?
But that is beside the mark. She never even began to toss when
her heart was whole.

And now she has carried the baby to bed. I hear her soft,
deliberate steps moving between the dining-room and the kitchen,
there and back again, to the tune of the clattering dishes. And now
all is quiet. What is happening now? Oh, I know just as surely as
if I'd gone to see — she is standing in the middle of the kitchen
facing the rainy window. Her head is bent, with one finger she is
tracing something — nothing — on the table. It is cold in the
kitchen; the gas jumps; the tap drips; it's a forlorn picture. And
nobody is going to come behind her, to take her in his arms, to
kiss her soft hair, to lead her to the fire and rub her hands warm
again. Nobody is going to call her or to wonder what she is doing
out there. And she knows it. And yet, being a woman, deep down,
deep down, she really does expect the miracle to happen; she really
could embrace that dark, dark deceit, rather than live — like this.

II

To live like this. . . . I write those words very carefully, very beautifully. For some reason I feel inclined to sign them, or to write
underneath — Trying a New Pen. But, seriously, isn't it staggering
to think what may be contained in one innocent-looking little
phrase? It tempts me — it tempts me terribly. Scene: The supper-
table. My wife has just handed me my tea. I stir it, lift the spoon,
idly chase and then carefully capture a speck of tea-leaf, and
having brought it ashore, I murmur, quite gently, "How long shall
we continue to live — like — this?" And immediately there is that
famous "blinding flash and deafening roar. Huge pieces of débris
(I must say I like débris) are flung into the air . . . and when the
dark clouds of smoke have drifted away . . ." But this will never

happen; I shall never know it. It will be found upon me "intact," as they say. "Open my heart and you will see . . ."

Why? Ah, there you have me! There is the most difficult question of all to answer. Why do people stay together? Putting aside "for the sake of the children", and "the habit of years" and "economic reasons" as lawyers' nonsense — it's not much more — if one really does try to find out why it is that people don't leave each other, one discovers a mystery. It is because they can't; they are bound. And nobody on earth knows what are the bonds that bind them except those two. Am I being obscure? Well, the thing itself isn't so frightfully crystal clear, is it? Let me put it like this. Supposing you are taken, absolutely, first into his confidence and then into hers. Supposing you know all there is to know about the situation. And having given it not only your deepest sympathy but your most honest impartial criticism, you declare, very calmly (but not without the slightest suggestion of relish — for there is — I swear there is — in the very best of us — something that leaps up and cries "A-ahh!" for joy at the thought of destroying), "Well, my opinion is that you two people ought to part. You'll do no earthly good together. Indeed, it seems to me, it's the duty of either to set the other free." What happens then? He — and she — agree. It is their conviction too. You are only saying what they have been thinking all last night. And away they go to act on your advice, immediately. . . . And the next time you hear of them they are still together. You see — you've reckoned without the unknown quantity — which is their secret relation to each other — and that they can't disclose even if they want to. Thus far you may tell and no further. Oh, don't misunderstand me! It need not necessarily have anything to do with their sleeping together. . . . But this brings me to a thought I've often half entertained. Which is that human beings, as we know them, don't choose each other at all. It is the owner, the second self inhabiting them, who makes the choice for his own particular purposes, and — this may sound absurdly far-fetched — it's the second self in the other which responds. Dimly — dimly — or so it has seemed to me — we realise this, at any rate to the extent that we realise the hopelessness of trying to escape. So that, what it all amounts to is — if the impermanent selves of my wife and me are happy — *tant mieux pour nous* — if miserable — *tant pis*. . . . But I don't know, I don't know. And it may be that it's something entirely individual in me — this sensation (yes, it is even a sensation) of how extraordinarily *shell-like* we are as we are — little creatures, peering out of the sentry-box at the gate, ogling through our glass case at the entry, wan little servants, who never can say for certain, even, if the master is out or in. . . .

The door opens . . . My wife. She says, "I am going to bed."

And I look up vaguely, and vaguely say, "You are going to bed."

"Yes." A tiny pause. "Don't forget — will you? — to turn out the gas in the hall."

And again I repeat, "The gas in the hall."

There was a time — the time before — when this habit of mine — it really has become a habit now — it wasn't one then — was one of our sweetest jokes together. It began, of course, when on several occasions I really was deeply engaged and I didn't hear. I emerged only to see her shaking her head and laughing at me, "You haven't heard a word!"

"No. What did you say?"

Why should she think that so funny and charming? She did — it delighted her. "Oh, my darling, it's so like you! It's so — so —" And I knew she loved me for it. I knew she positively looked forward to coming in and disturbing me, and so — as one does — I played up. I was guaranteed to be wrapped away every evening at 10.30 p.m. But now? For some reason I feel it would be crude to stop my performance. It's simplest to play on. But what is she waiting for tonight? Why doesn't she go? Why prolong this? She is going. No, her hand on the door-knob, she turns round again, and she says in the most curious, small, breathless voice, "You're not cold?"

Oh, it's not fair to be as pathetic as that! That was simply damnable. I shuddered all over before I managed to bring out a slow "No-o!" while my left hand ruffles the reference pages.

She is gone; she will not come back again tonight. It is not only I who recognise that — the room changes too. It relaxes, like an old actor. Slowly the mask is rubbed off; the look of strained attention changes to an air of heavy, sullen brooding. Every line, every fold breathes fatigue. The mirror is quenched; the ash whitens; only my sly lamp burns on. . . . But what a cynical indifference to me it all shows! Or should I perhaps be flattered? No, we understand each other. You know those stories of little children who are suckled by wolves and accepted by the tribe, and how for ever after they move freely among their fleet, grey brothers? Something like that has happened to me. But wait! That about the wolves won't do. Curious! Before I wrote it down, while it was still in my head, I was delighted with it. It seemed to express, and more, to suggest, just what I wanted to say. But written, I can smell the falseness

immediately and the . . . source of the smell is in that word fleet.
Don't you agree? Fleet, grey brothers! "Fleet." A word I never use.
When I wrote "wolves" it skimmed across my mind like a shadow
and I couldn't resist it. Tell me! Tell me! Why is it so difficult to
write simply — and not simply only but *sotto voce*, if you know
what I mean? That is how I long to write. No fine effects — no bra-
vura. But just the plain truth, as only a liar can tell it.

III

I light a cigarette, lean back, inhale deeply — and find myself wondering if my wife is asleep. Or is she lying in her cold bed, staring
into the dark, with those trustful, bewildered eyes? Her eyes are
like the eyes of a cow that is being driven along a road. "Why am
I being driven — what harm have I done?" But I really am not
responsible for that look; it's her natural expression. One day,
when she was turning out a cupboard, she found a little old photograph of herself, taken when she was a girl at school. In her con-
firmation dress, she explained. And there were the eyes, even
then. I remember saying to her, "Did you always look so sad?"
Leaning over my shoulder, she laughed lightly. "Do I look sad?"
I think it's just . . . me." And she waited for me to say something
about it. But I was marvelling at her courage at having shown it
to me at all. It was a hideous photograph! And I wondered again
if she realised how plain she was, and comforted herself with the
idea that people who loved each other didn't criticise but accepted
everything, or if she really rather liked her appearance and
expected me to say something complimentary.

Oh, that was base of me! How could I have forgotten all the
numberless times when I have known her turn away to avoid the
light, press her face into my shoulders. And, above all, how could
I have forgotten the afternoon of our wedding-day when we sat on
the green bench in the Botanical Gardens and listened to the
band; how, in an interval between two pieces, she suddenly turned
to me and said in the voice in which one says, "Do you think the
grass is damp?" or "Do you think it's time for tea?" . . . "Tell me,
do you think physical beauty is so very important?" I don't like to
think how often she had rehearsed that question. And do you
know what I answered? At that moment, as if at my command,
there came a great gush of hard, bright sound from the band, and
I managed to shout above it cheerfully, "I didn't hear what you
said." Devilish! Wasn't it? Perhaps not wholly. She looked like the

poor patient who hears the surgeon say, "It will certainly be necessary to perform the operation — but not now!"

IV

But all this conveys the impression that my wife and I were never really happy together. Not true! Not true! We were marvellously, radiantly happy. We were a model couple. If you had seen us together, any time, any place, if you had followed us, tracked us down, spied, taken us off our guard, you still would have been forced to confess, "I have never seen a more ideally suited pair." Until last autumn.

But really to explain what happened then I should have to go back and back — I should have to dwindle until my tiny hands clutched the banisters, the stair-rail was higher than my head, and I peered through to watch my father padding softly up and down. There were coloured windows on the landings. As he came up, first his bald head was scarlet, then it was yellow. How frightened I was! And when they put me to bed, it was to dream that we were living inside one of my father's big coloured bottles. For he was a chemist. I was born nine years after my parents were married. I was an only child, and the effort to produce even me — small, withered bud I must have been — sapped all my mother's strength. She never left her room again. Bed, sofa, window, she moved between the three. Well I can see her, on the window days, sitting, her cheek in her hand, staring out. Her room looked over the street. Opposite there was a wall plastered with advertisements for travelling shows and circuses and so on. I stand beside her, and we gaze at the slim lady in a red dress hitting a dark gentleman over the head with her parasol, or at the tiger peering through the jungle while the clown, close by, balances a bottle on his nose, or at a little golden-haired girl sitting on the knee of an old black man in a broad cotton hat. . . . She says nothing. On sofa days there is a flannel dressing-gown that I loathe and a cushion that keeps on slipping off the hard sofa. I pick it up. It has flowers and writing sewn on. I ask what the writing says, and she whispers, "Sweet Repose!" In bed her fingers plait, in tight little plaits, the fringe of the quilt and her lips are thin. And that is all there is of my mother, except the last queer "episode" that comes later.

My father . . . Curled up in the corner on the lid of a round box that held sponges, I stared at my father so long, it's as though his image, cut off at the waist by the counter, has remained solid in my memory. Perfectly bald, polished head, shaped like a thin egg, creased, creamy cheeks, little bags under the eyes, large pale ears like handles. His manner was discreet, sly, faintly amused and tinged with impudence. Long before I could appreciate it I knew the mixture . . . I even used to copy him in my corner, bending forward, with a small reproduction of his faint sneer. In the evening his customers were, chiefly, young women; some of them came in every day for his famous fivepenny pick-me-up. Their gaudy looks, their voices, their free ways fascinated me. I longed to be my father, handing them across the counter the little glass of bluish stuff they tossed off so greedily. God knows what it was made of. Years after I drank some, just to see what it tasted like, and I felt as though someone had given me a terrific blow on the head; I felt stunned.

One of those evenings I remember vividly. It was cold; it must have been autumn, for the flaring gas was lighted after my tea. I sat in my corner and my father was mixing something; the shop was empty. Suddenly the bell jangled and a young woman rushed in, crying so loud, sobbing so hard, that it didn't sound real. She wore a green cape trimmed with fur and a hat with cherries dangling. My father came from behind the screen. But she couldn't stop herself at first. She stood in the middle of the shop and wrung her hands and moaned; I've never heard such crying since. Presently she managed to gasp out, "Give me a pick-me-up!" Then she drew a long breath, trembled away from him and quavered, "I've had *bad news!*" And in the flaring gaslight I saw the whole side of her face was puffed up and purple; her lip was cut and her eyelid looked as though it was gummed fast over the wet eye. My father pushed the glass across the counter, and she took the purse out of her stocking and paid him. But she couldn't drink; clutching the glass, she stared in front of her as if she could not believe what she saw. Each time she put her head back the tears spurted out again. Finally she put the glass down. It was no use. Holding the cape with one hand, she ran in the same way out of the shop again. My father gave no sign. But long after she had gone I crouched in my corner, and when I think back it's as though I felt my whole body vibrating — "So that's what it is outside," I thought. "That's what it's like out there."

V

Do you remember your childhood? I am always coming across these marvellous accounts by writers who declare that they remember "everything". I certainly don't. The dark stretches, the blanks, are much bigger than the bright glimpses. I seem to have spent most of my time like a plant in a cupboard. Now and again, when the sun shone, a careless hand thrust me out on to the window-sill, and a careless hand whipped me in again — and that was all. But what happened in the darkness — I wonder? Did one grow? Pale stem . . . timid leaves . . . white reluctant bud. No wonder I was hated at school. Even the masters shrank from me. I somehow knew that my soft, hesitating voice disgusted them. I knew, too, how they turned away from my shocked, staring eyes. I was small and thin and I smelled of the shop; my nickname was Gregory Powder. School was a tin building, stuck on the raw hillside. There were dark red streaks like blood in the oozing clay banks of the playground. I hide in the passage, where the coats hang, and am discovered there by one of the masters. "What are you doing there in the dark?" His terrible voice kills me; I die before his eyes. I am standing in a ring of thrust-out heads; some are grinning, some look greedy, some are spitting. And it is always cold. Big crushed-up clouds press across the sky; the rusty water in the school tank is frozen; the bell sounds numb. One day they put a dead bird in my overcoat pocket. I found it just when I reached home. Oh, what a strange flutter there was at my heart when I drew out that terribly soft, cold little body, with the legs thin as pins and the claws wrung. I sat on the back door step in the yard and put the bird in my cap. The feathers round the neck looked wet and there was a tiny tuft just above the closed eyes that stood up too. How tightly the beak was shut! I could not see the mark where it was divided. I stretched out one wing and touched the soft, secret down underneath; I tried to make the claws curl round my little finger. But I didn't feel sorry for it — no! I wondered. The smoke from our kitchen chimney poured downwards, and flakes of soot floated — soft, light in the air. Through a big crack in the cement yard a poor-looking plant with dull, reddish flowers had pushed its way. I looked at the dead bird again. . . . And that is the first time that I remember singing — rather . . . listening to a silent voice inside a little cage that was me.

VI

But what has all this to do with my married happiness? How can all this affect my wife and me? Why — to tell what happened last autumn — do I run all this way back into the Past? The Past —

what is the Past? I might say the star-shaped flake of soot on a leaf of the poor-looking plant, and the bird lying on the quilted lining of my cap, and my father's pestle and my mother's cushion belong to it. But that is not to say they are any less mine than they were when I looked upon them with my very eyes and touched them with these fingers. No, they are more — they are a living part of me. Who am I, in fact, as I sit here at this table, but my own past? If I deny that, I am nothing. And if I were to try to divide my life into childhood, youth, early manhood and so on, it would be a kind of affectation; I should know I was doing it just because of the pleasantly important sensation it gives one to rule lines and to use green ink for childhood, red for the next stage, and purple for the period of adolescence. For, one thing I have learnt, one thing I do believe is, Nothing Happens Suddenly. Yes, that is my religion, I suppose.

My mother's death, for instance. Is it more distant from me today than it was then? It is just as close, as strange, as puzzling, and, in spite of all the countless times I have recalled the circumstances, I know no more now than I did then whether I dreamed them or whether they really occurred. It happened when I was thirteen and I slept in a little strip of a room on what was called the half-landing. One night I woke up with a start to see my mother, in her nightgown, without even the hated flannel dressing-gown, sitting on my bed. But the strange thing which frightened me was, she wasn't looking at me. Her head was bent; the short, thin trail of hair lay between her shoulders; her hands were pressed between her knees and my bed shook; she was shivering. It was the first time I had ever seen her out of her own room. I said, or I think I said, "Is that you, Mother?" And as she turned round, I saw in the moonlight how queer she looked. Her face looked small — quite different. She looked like one of the boys at the school baths, who sits on a step, shivering just like that, and wants to go in and yet is frightened.

"Are you awake?" she said. Her eyes opened; I think she smiled. She leaned towards me. "I've been poisoned," she whispered. "Your father's poisoned me." And she nodded. Then, before I could say a word, she was gone; I thought I heard the door shut. I sat quite still, I couldn't move, I think I expected something else to happen. For a long time I listened for something; there wasn't a sound. The candle was by my bed, but I was too frightened to stretch out my hand for the matches. But even while I wondered what I ought to do, even while my heart thumped — everything became confused. I lay down and pulled the blankets round me, I fell asleep, and the next morning my mother was found dead of failure of the heart.

Did that visit happen? Was it a dream? Why did she come to tell me? Or why, if she came, did she go away so quickly? And her expression — so joyous under the frightened look — was that real? I believed it fully the afternoon of the funeral, when I saw my father dressed up for his part, hat and all. That tall hat so gleaming black and round was like a cork covered with black sealing-wax, and the rest of my father was awfully like a bottle, with his face for the label — *Deadly Poison*. It flashed into my mind as I stood opposite him in the hall. And Deadly Poison, or old D.P., was my private name for him from that day.

VII

Late, it grows late. I love the night. I love to feel the tide of darkness rising slowly and slowly washing, turning over and over, lifting, floating, all that lies strewn upon the dark beach, all that lies hid in rocky hollows. I love, I love this strange feeling of drifting — whither? After my mother's death I hated to go to bed. I used to sit on the window-sill, folded up, and watch the sky. It seemed to me the moon moved much faster than the sun. And one big, bright green star I chose for my own. My star! But I never thought of it beckoning to me or twinkling merrily for my sake. Cruel, indifferent, splendid — it burned in the airy night. No matter — it was mine! But, growing close up against the window, there was a creeper with small, bunched-up pink and purple flowers. These did know me. These, when I touched them at night, welcomed my fingers; the little tendrils, so weak, so delicate, knew I would not hurt them. When the wind moved the leaves I felt I understood their shaking. When I came to the window, it seemed to me the flowers said among themselves, "The boy is here."

As the months passed, there was often a light in my father's room below. And I heard voices and laughter. "He's got some woman with him," I thought. But it meant nothing to me. Then the gay voice, the sound of the laughter, gave me the idea it was one of the girls who used to come to the shop in the evenings — and gradually I began to imagine which girl it was. It was the dark one in the red coat and skirt who once had given me a penny. A merry face stooped over me — warm breath tickled my neck — there were little beads of black on her long lashes, and when she opened her arms to kiss me there came a marvellous wave of scent! Yes, that was the one.

Time passed, and I forgot the moon and my green star and my shy creeper — I came to the window to wait for the light in my father's window, to listen for the laughing voice, until one night I dozed and I dreamed she came again — again she drew me to her, something soft, scented, warm and merry hung over me like a cloud. But when I tried to see, her eyes only mocked me, her red lips opened and she hissed, "Little sneak! Little sneak!" But not as if she were angry, as if she understood, and her smile somehow was like a rat — hateful!

The night after, I lighted the candle and sat down at the table instead. By and by, as the flame steadied, there was a small lake of liquid wax, surrounded by a white, smooth wall. I took a pin and made little holes in this wall and then sealed them up faster than the wax could escape. After a time I fancied the candle flame joined in the game; it leapt up, quivered, wagged; it even seemed to laugh. But while I played with the candle and smiled and broke off the tiny white peaks of wax that rose above the wall and floated them on my lake, a feeling of awful dreariness fastened on me — yes, that's the word. It crept up from my knees to my thighs, into my arms; I ached all over with misery. And I felt so strangely that I couldn't move. Something bound me there by the table — I couldn't even let the pin drop that I held between my finger and thumb. For a moment I came to a stop, as it were.

Then the shrivelled case of the bud split and fell, the plant in the cupboard came into flower. "Who am I?" I thought. "What is all this?" And I looked at my room, at the broken bust of the man called Hahnemann on top of the cupboard, at my little bed with the pillow like an envelope. I saw it all, but not as I had seen before. . . . Everything lived, everything. But that was not all. I was equally alive and — it's the only way I can express it — the barriers were down between us — I had come into my own world!

VIII

The barriers were down. I had been all my life a little outcast; but until that moment no one had "accepted" me; I had lain in the cupboard — or the cave forlorn. But now I was taken, I was accepted, claimed. I did not consciously turn away from the world of human beings, I had never known it; but I from that night did beyond words consciously turn towards my silent brothers. . . .

The Doves' Nest

I

AFTER LUNCH Milly and her mother were sitting as usual on the balcony beyond the salon admiring for the five-hundredth time the stocks, the roses, the small, bright grass beneath the palms, and the oranges against a wavy line of blue, when a card was brought them by Marie. Visitors at the Villa Martin were very rare. True, the English clergyman, Mr Sandiman, had called, and he had come a second time with his wife to tea. But an awful thing had happened on that second occasion. Mother had made a mistake. She had said "More tea, Mr Sandybags?" Oh, what a frightful thing to have happened! How could she have done it? Milly still flamed at the thought. And he had evidently not forgiven them; he'd never come again. So this card put them both into quite a flutter.

Mr *Walter Prodger*, they read. And then an American address, so very much abbreviated that neither of them understood it. Walter Prodger? But they'd never heard of him. Mother looked from the card to Milly.

"Prodger, dear?" she asked mildly, as though helping Milly to a slice of never-before-tasted pudding.

And Milly seemed to be holding her plate back in the way she answered "I — don't — know, Mother."

"These are the occasions," said Mother, becoming a little flustered, "when one does so feel the need of our dear English servants. Now if I could just say, 'What is he like, Annie?' I should know whether to see him or not. But he may be some common man, selling something — one of those American inventions for peeling things, you know, dear. Or he may even be some kind of foreign sharper." Mother winced at the hard, bright little word as though she had given herself a dig with her embroidery scissors.

But here Marie smiled at Milly and murmured, "*C'est un très beau Monsieur.*"

"What does she say, dear?"

"She says he looks very nice, Mother."

"Well, we'd better — " began Mother. "Where is he now, I wonder."

Marie answered "In the vestibule, Madame."

In the hall! Mother jumped up, seriously alarmed. In the hall, with all those valuable little foreign things that didn't belong to them scattered over the tables.

"Show him in, Marie. Come, Milly, come, dear. We will see him in the salon. Oh, why isn't Miss Anderson here?" almost wailed Mother.

But Miss Anderson, Mother's new companion, never was on the spot when she was wanted. She had been engaged to be a comfort, a support to them both. Fond of travelling, a cheerful disposition, a good packer and so on. And then, when they had come all this way and taken the Villa Martin and moved in, she had turned out to be a Roman Catholic. Half her time, more than half, was spent wearing out the knees of her skirts in cold churches. It was really too . . .

The door opened. A middle-aged, clean-shaven, very well-dressed stranger stood bowing before them. His bow was stately. Milly saw it pleased Mother very much; she bowed her Queen Alexandra bow back. As for Milly, she never could bow. She smiled, feeling shy, but deeply interested.

"Have I the pleasure," said the stranger very courteously, with a strong American accent, "of speaking with Mrs Wyndham Fawcett?"

"I am Mrs Fawcett," said Mother graciously, "and this is my daughter, Mildred."

"Pleased to meet you, Miss Fawcett." And the stranger shot a fresh, chill hand at Milly, who grasped it just in time before it was gone again.

"Won't you sit down?" said Mother, and she waved faintly at all the gilt chairs.

"Thank you, I will," said the stranger.

Down he sat, still solemn, crossing his legs and, most surprisingly, his arms as well. His face looked at them over his dark arms as over a gate.

"Milly, sit down, dear."

So Milly sat down, too, on the Madame Récamier couch and traced a filet lace flower with her finger. There was a little pause. She saw the stranger swallow; Mother's fan opened and shut.

Then he said, "I took the liberty of calling, Mrs Fawcett, because

I had the pleasure of your husband's acquaintance in the States when he was lecturing there some years ago. I should like very much to renoo our — well — I venture to hope we might call it friendship. Is he with you at present? Are you expecting him out? I noticed his name was not mentioned in the local paper. But I put that down to a foreign custom, perhaps — giving precedence to the lady."

And here the stranger looked as though he might be going to smile.

But as a matter of fact it was extremely awkward. Mother's mouth shook. Milly squeezed her hands between her knees, but she watched hard from under her eyebrows. Good, noble little Mummy! How Milly admired her as she heard her say, gently and quite simply, "I am sorry to say my husband died two years ago."

Mr Prodger gave a great start. "Did he?" He thrust out his under lip, frowned, pondered. "I am truly sorry to hear that, Mrs Fawcett. I hope you'll believe me when I say I had no idea your husband had . . . passed over."

"Of course." Mother softly stroked her skirt.

"I do trust," said Mr Prodger, more seriously still, "that my inquiry didn't give you too much pain."

"No, no. It's quite all right," said the gentle voice.

But Mr Prodger insisted. "You're sure? You're positive?"

At that Mother raised her head and gave him one of her still, bright, exalted glances that Milly knew so well. "I'm not in the least hurt," she said, as one might say it from the midst of the fiery furnace.

Mr Prodger looked relieved. He changed his attitude and continued. "I hope this regrettable circumstance will not deprive me of your —"

"Oh, certainly not. We shall be delighted. We are always so pleased to know anyone who —" Mother gave a little bound, a little flutter. She flew from her shadowy branch on to a sunny one. "Is this your first visit to the Riviera?"

"It is," said Mr Prodger. "The fact is I was in Florence until recently. But I took a heavy cold there —"

"Florence so damp," cooed Mother.

"And the doctor recommended I should come here for the sunshine before I started for home."

"The sun is so very lovely here," agreed Mother enthusiastically.

"Well, I don't think we get too much of it," said Mr Prodger dubiously, and two lines showed at his lips. "I seem to have been sitting around in my hotel more days than I care to count."

"Ah, hotels are so very trying," said Mother, and she drooped sympathetically at the thought of a lonely man in an hotel. . . . "You are alone here?" she asked gently, just in case . . . one never knew . . . it was better to be on the safe, the tactful side.

But her fears were groundless.

"Oh yes, I'm alone," cried Mr Prodger, more heartily than he had spoken yet, and he took a speck of thread off his immaculate trouser leg. Something in his voice puzzled Milly. What was it?

"Still, the scenery is so very beautiful," said Mother, "that one really does not feel the need of friends. I was only saying to my daughter yesterday I could live here for years without going outside the garden gate. It is all so beautiful."

"Is that so?" said Mr Prodger soberly. He added, "You have a very charming villa." And he glanced round the salon. "Is all this antique furniture genuine, may I ask?"

"I believe so," said Mother. "I was certainly given to understand it was. Yes, we love our villa. But, of course, it is very large for two, that is to say three, ladies. My companion, Miss Anderson, is with us. But unfortunately she is a Roman Catholic and so she is out most of the time."

Mr Prodger bowed as one who agreed that Roman Catholics were very seldom in.

"But I am so fond of space," continued Mother, "and so is my daughter. We both love large rooms and plenty of them — don't we, Milly?"

This time Mr Prodger looked at Milly quite cordially and remarked, "Yes, young people like plenty of room to run about."

He got up, put one hand behind his back, slapped the other upon it and went over to the balcony.

"You've a view of the sea from here," he observed.

The ladies might well have noticed it; the whole Mediterranean swung before the windows.

"We are so fond of the sea," said Mother, getting up too.

Mr Prodger looked towards Milly. "Do you see those yachts, Miss Fawcett?"

Milly saw them.

"Do you happen to know what they're doing?" asked Mr Prodger.

What they were doing? What a funny question! Milly stared and bit her lip.

"They're racing!" said Mr Prodger, and this time he did actually smile at her.

"Oh yes, of course," stammered Milly. "Of course they are." She knew that.

"Well, they're not always at it," said Mr Prodger good-humouredly. And he turned to Mother and began to take a ceremonious farewell.

"I wonder," hesitated Mother, folding her little hands and eyeing him, "if you would care to lunch with us? — if you would not be too dull with two ladies. We should be so very pleased."

Mr Prodger became intensely serious again. He seemed to brace himself to meet the luncheon invitation. "Thank you very much, Mrs Fawcett. I should be delighted."

"That will be very nice," said Mother warmly. "Let me see. Today is Monday — isn't it, Milly? Would Wednesday suit you?"

Mr Prodger replied, "It would suit me excellently to lunch with you on Wednesday, Mrs Fawcett. At *mee-dee*, I presume, as they call it here."

"Oh no! We keep our English times. At one o'clock," said Mother.

And that being arranged, Mr Prodger became more and more ceremonious and bowed himself out of the room.

Mother rang for Marie to look after him, and a moment later the big glass hall-door shut.

"Well!" said Mother. She was all smiles. Little smiles, like butterflies, alighting on her lips and gone again. "That was an adventure, Milly, wasn't it, dear? And I thought he was such a very charming man, didn't you?"

Milly made a little face at Mother and rubbed her eyes.

"Of course you did. You must have, dear. And his appearance was so satisfactory — wasn't it?" Mother was obviously enraptured. "I mean he looked so very well kept. Did you notice his hands? Every nail shone like a diamond. I must say I do like to see . . ."

She broke off. She came over to Milly and patted her big collar straight.

"You do think it was right of me to ask him to lunch — don't you, dear?" said Mother pathetically.

Mother made her feel so big, so tall. But she was tall. She could pick Mother up in her arms. Sometimes, rare moods came when she did. Swooped on Mother who squeaked like a mouse and even kicked. But not lately. Very seldom now. . . .

"It was so strange," said Mother. There was the still, bright, exalted glance again. "I suddenly seemed to hear Father say to me 'Ask him to lunch.' And then there was some — warning. . . . I think it was about the wine. But that I didn't catch — very unfortunately," she added mournfully. She put her hand on her breast, she bowed her head. "Father is still so near," she whispered.

Milly looked out of the window. She hated Mother going on like this. But, of course, she couldn't say anything. Out of the window there was the sea and the sunlight silver on the palms, like water dripping from silver oars. Milly felt a yearning — what was it? — it was like a yearning to fly.

But Mother's voice brought her back to the salon, to the gilt chairs, the gilt couches, sconces, cabinets, the tables with the heavy-sweet flowers, the faded brocade, the pink-spotted Chinese dragons on the mantelpiece and the two Turks' heads in the fireplace that supported the broad logs.

"I think a leg of lamb would be nice, don't you, dear?" said Mother. "The lamb is so very small and delicate just now. And men like nothing so much as plain roast meat. Yvonne prepares it so nicely, too, with that little frill of paper lace round the top of the leg. It always reminds me of something — I can't think what. But it certainly makes it look very attractive indeed."

II

Wednesday came. And the flutter that Mother and Milly had felt over the visiting-card extended to the whole villa. Yes, it was not too much to say that the whole villa thrilled and fluttered at the idea of having a man to lunch. Old, flat-footed Yvonne came waddling back from market with a piece of gorgonzola in so perfect a condition that when she found Marie in the kitchen she flung down her great basket, snatched the morsel up and held it, rustling in its paper, to her quivering bosom.

"*J'ai trouvé un morceau de gorgonzola*," she panted, rolling up her eyes as though she invited the heavens themselves to look down upon it. "*J'ai un morceau de gorgonzola ici pour un prr-ince, ma fille.*" And hissing the word "*prr-ince*" like lightning, she thrust the morsel under Marie's nose. Marie, who was a delicate creature, almost swooned at the shock.

"Do you think," cried Yvonne scornfully, "that I would ever buy such cheese *pour ces dames?* Never. Never. *Jamais de ma vie.*" Her sausage finger wagged before her nose, and she minced in a dreadful imitation of Mother's French, "We have none of us large appetites, Yvonne. We are very fond of boiled eggs and mashed potatoes and a nice, plain salad. Ah-Bah!" With a snort of contempt she flung away her shawl, rolled up her sleeves, and began unpacking the basket. At the bottom there was a flat bottle which, sighing, she laid aside.

"*De quoi pour mes cors,*" said she.

And Marie, seizing a bottle of Sauterne and bearing it off to the dining-room, murmured as she shut the kitchen door behind her, "*Et voilà pour les cors de Monsieur!*"

The dining-room was a large room panelled in dark wood. It had a massive mantelpiece and carved chairs covered in crimson damask. On the heavy, polished table stood an oval glass dish decorated with little gilt swags. This dish, which it was Marie's duty to keep filled with fresh flowers, fascinated her. The sight of it gave her a *frisson*. It reminded her always, as it lay solitary on the dark expanse, of a little tomb. And one day, passing through the long windows on to the stone terrace and down the steps into the garden, she had the happy thought of so arranging the flowers that they would be appropriate to one of the ladies on a future tragic occasion. Her first creation had been terrible. *Tomb of Mademoiselle Anderson* in black pansies, lily-of-the-valley and a frill of heliotrope. It gave her a most intense, curious pleasure to hand Miss Anderson the potatoes at lunch and at the same time to gaze beyond her at her triumph. It was like (O *ciel!*) — it was like handing potatoes to a corpse.

The *Tomb of Madame* was, on the contrary, almost gay. Foolish little flowers, half yellow, half blue, hung over the edge, wisps of green trailed across and in the middle there was a large scarlet rose. *Coeur saignant*, Marie had called it. But it did not look in the least like a *coeur saignant*. It looked flushed and cheerful, like Mother emerging from the luxury of a warm bath.

Milly's, of course, was all white. White stocks, little white rose-buds, with a sprig or two of dark box edging. It was Mother's favourite.

Poor innocent! Marie, at the sideboard, had to turn her back when she heard Mother exclaim, "Isn't it pretty, Milly? Isn't it sweetly pretty? Most artistic. So original." And she had said to Marie, "*C'est très joli, Marie. Très original.*"

Marie's smile was so remarkable that Milly, peeling a tangerine, remarked to Mother, "I don't think she likes you to admire them. It makes her uncomfortable."

But today — the glory of her opportunity made Marie feel quite faint as she seized her flower scissors. *Tombeau d'un beau Monsieur.* She was forbidden to cut the orchids that grew round the fountain basin. But what were orchids for if not for such an occasion? Her fingers trembled as the scissors snipped away. They were enough; Marie added two small sprays of palm. And back in the dining-room she had the happy idea of binding the palm together with a twist of gold thread deftly torn off the fringe of the dining-room curtains. The effect was superb. Marie almost seemed to see her *beau Monsieur*, very small, very small, at the bottom of the bowl, in full evening dress with a ribbon across his chest and his ears white as wax.

What surprised Milly, however, was that Miss Anderson should pay any attention to Mr Prodger's coming. She rustled to breakfast in her best black silk blouse, her Sunday blouse, with the large, painful-looking crucifix dangling over the front. Milly was alone when Miss Anderson entered the dining-room. This was unfortunate, for she always tried to avoid being left alone with Miss Anderson. She could not say exactly why; it was a feeling. She had the feeling that Miss Anderson might say something about God, or something fearfully intimate. Oh, she would sink through the floor if such a thing happened; she would expire. Supposing she were to say "Milly, do you believe in our Lord?" Heavens! It simply didn't bear thinking about.

"Good morning, my dear," said Miss Anderson, and her fingers, cold, pale, like church candles, touched Milly's cheeks.

"Good morning, Miss Anderson. May I give you some coffee?" said Milly, trying to be natural.

"Thank you, dear child," said Miss Anderson, and laughing her light, nervous laugh, she hooked on her eyeglasses and stared at the basket of rolls. "And is it today that you expect your guest?" she asked.

Now why did she ask that? Why pretend when she knew perfectly well? That was all part of her strangeness. Or was it because she wanted to be friendly? Miss Anderson was more than friendly; she was genial. But there was always this something. Was she spying? People said at school that Roman Catholics spied. . . . Miss Anderson rustled, rustled about the house like a dead leaf. Now she was on the stairs, now in the upstairs passage. Sometimes, at night, when Milly was feverish she woke up and heard that rustle outside her door. Was Miss Anderson looking through the keyhole? And one night she actually had the idea that Miss Anderson had bored two holes in the wall above her head and was watching her from there. The feeling was so strong that next time she went into Miss Anderson's room her eyes flew to the spot. To her horror a large picture hung there. Had it been there before? . . .

"Guest?" The crisp breakfast roll broke in half at the word.

"Yes, I think it is," said Milly vaguely, and her blue, flower-like eyes were raised to Miss Anderson in a vague stare.

"It will make quite a little change in our little party," said the much-too-pleasant voice. "I confess I miss very much the society of men. I have had such a great deal of it in my life. I think that ladies by themselves are apt to get a little — h'm — h'm . . ." And helping herself to cherry jam, she spilt it on the cloth.

Milly took a large, childish bite out of her roll. There was nothing to reply to this. But how young Miss Anderson made her feel! She made her want to be naughty, to pour milk over her head or make a noise with a spoon.

"Ladies by themselves," went on Miss Anderson, who realised none of this, "are very apt to find their interests limited."

"Why?" said Milly, goaded to reply. People always said that; it sounded most unfair.

"I think," said Miss Anderson, taking off her eyeglasses and looking a little dim, "it is the absence of political discussion."

"Oh, politics!" cried Milly airily. "I hate politics. Father always said —" But here she pulled up short. She crimsoned. She didn't want to talk about Father to Miss Anderson.

"Oh! Look! Look! A butterfly!" cried Miss Anderson, softly and hastily. "Look, what a darling!" Her own cheeks flushed a slow red at the sight of the darling butterfly fluttering so softly over the glittering table.

That was very nice of Miss Anderson — fearfully nice of her. She must have realised that Milly didn't want to talk about Father and so she had mentioned the butterfly on purpose. Milly smiled at Miss Anderson as she never had smiled at her before. And she said in her warm, youthful voice, "He is a duck, isn't he? I love butterflies. I think they are great lambs."

III

The morning whisked away as foreign mornings do. Mother had half decided to wear her hat at lunch.

"What do you think, Milly? Do you think as head of the house it might be appropriate? On the other hand, one does not want to do anything at all extreme."

"Which do you mean, Mother? Your mushroom or the jampot?"

"Oh, not the jampot, dear." Mother was quite used to Milly's name for it. "I somehow don't feel myself in a hat without a brim. And to tell you the truth, I am still not quite certain whether I was wise in buying a jampot. I cannot help the feeling that if I were to meet Father in it he would be a little too surprised. More than once lately," went on Mother quickly, "I have thought of taking off the trimming, turning it upside down and making it into a nice little work-bag. What do you think, dear? But we must not go into it now, Milly. This is not the moment for such schemes. Come on to the balcony. I have told Marie we shall have coffee there. What about bringing out that big chair with the nice, substantial legs for Mr Prodger? Men are so fond of nice, substantial . . . No, not by yourself, love! Let me help you."

When the chair was carried out Milly thought it looked exactly like Mr Prodger. It *was* Mr Prodger admiring the view.

"No, don't sit down on it. You mustn't," she cried hastily, as Mother began to subside. She put her arm through Mother's and drew her back into the salon.

Happily, at that moment there was a rustle and Miss Anderson was upon them. In excellent time, for once. She carried a copy of the *Morning Post*.

"I have been trying to find out from this," said she, lightly tapping the newspaper with her eyeglasses, "whether Congress is sitting at present. But unfortunately, after reading my copy right through, I happened to glance at the heading and discovered it was five weeks old."

Congress! Would Mr Prodger expect them to talk about Congress? The idea terrified Mother. Congress! The American parliament, of course, composed of senators — grey-bearded old men in frock-coats and turn-down collars, rather like missionaries. But she did not feel at all competent to discuss them.

"I think we had better not be too intellectual," she suggested timidly, fearful of disappointing Miss Anderson, but more fearful still of the alternative.

"Still, one likes to be prepared," said Miss Anderson. And after a pause she added softly, "One never knows."

Ah, how true that was! One never does. Miss Anderson and Mother seemed both to ponder this truth. They sat silent, with head bent, as though listening to the whisper of the words.

"One never knows," said the pink-spotted dragons on the

mantelpiece and the Turks' heads pondered. Nothing is known — nothing. Everybody just waits for things to happen as they were waiting there for the stranger who came walking towards them through the sun and shadow under the budding plane trees, or driving, perhaps, in one of the small, cotton-covered cabs. . . . An angel passed over the Villa Martin. In that moment of hovering silence something timid, something beseeching seemed to lift, seemed to offer itself, as the flowers in the salon, uplifted, gave themselves to the light.

Then Mother said, "I hope Mr Prodger will not find the scent of the mimosa too powerful. Men are not fond of flowers in a room as a rule. I have heard it causes actual hay-fever in some cases. What do you think, Milly? Ought we perhaps — " But there was no time to do anything. A long, firm trill sounded from the hall door. It was a trill so calm and composed and unlike the tentative little push they gave the bell that it brought them back to the seriousness of the moment. They heard a man's voice; the door clicked shut again. He was inside. A stick rattled on the table. There was a pause, and then the door handle of the salon turned and Marie, in frilled muslin cuffs and an apron shaped like a heart, ushered in Mr Prodger.

Only Mr Prodger, after all? But whom had Milly expected to see? The feeling was there and gone again that she would not have been surprised to see somebody quite different, before she realised this wasn't quite the same Mr Prodger as before. He was smarter than ever: all brushed, combed, shining. The ears that Marie had seen white as wax flashed as if they had been pink enamelled. Mother fluttered up in her pretty little way, so hoping he had not found the heat of the day too trying to be out in . . . but happily it was a little early in the year for dust. Then Miss Anderson was introduced. Milly was ready this time for that fresh hand, but she almost gasped; it was so very chill. It was like a hand stretched out to you from the water. Then together they all sat down.

"Is this your first visit to the Riviera?" asked Miss Anderson graciously, dropping her handkerchief.

"It is," answered Mr Prodger composedly, and he folded his arms as before. "I was in Florence until recently, but I caught a heavy cold — "

"Florence so — " began Mother, when the beautiful brass gong, that burned like a fallen sun in the shadows of the hall, began to throb. First it was a low muttering, then it swelled, it quickened, it burst into a clash of triumph under Marie's sympathetic fingers.

Never had they been treated to such a performance before. Mr Prodger was all attention.

"That's a very fine gong," he remarked approvingly.

"We think it is so very oriental," said Mother. "It gives our little meals quite an Eastern flavour. Shall we . . ."

Their guest was at the door bowing.

"So many gentlemen and only one lady," fluttered Mother. "What I mean is the boot is on the other shoe. That is to say — come, Milly, come, dear." And she led the way to the dining-room.

Well, there they were. The cold, fresh napkins were shaken out of their charming shapes and Marie handed the omelette. Mr Prodger sat on Mother's right, facing Milly, and Miss Anderson had her back to the long windows. But after all — why should the fact of their having a man with them make such a difference? It did; it made all the difference. Why should they feel so stirred at the sight of that large hand outspread, moving among the wine glasses? Why should the sound of that loud, confident "Ah-hm!" change the very look of the dining-room? It was not a favourite room of theirs as a rule — it was overpowering. They bobbed uncertainly at the pale table with a curious feeling of exposure. They were like those meek guests who arrive unexpectedly at the fashionable hotel and are served with whatever may be ready, while the real luncheon, the real guests lurk important and contemptuous in the background. And although it was impossible for Marie to be other than deft, nimble and silent, what heart could she have in ministering to that most uninspiring of spectacles — three ladies dining alone?

Now all was changed. Marie filled their glasses to the brim as if to reward them for some marvellous feat of courage. These timid English ladies had captured a live lion, a real one, smelling faintly of eau-de-Cologne, and with a tip of handkerchief showing, white as a flake of snow.

"He is worthy of it," decided Marie, eyeing her orchids and palms.

Mr Prodger touched his hot plate with appreciative fingers.

"You'll hardly believe it, Mrs Fawcett," he remarked, turning to Mother, "but this is the first hot plate I've happened on since I left the States. I had begun to believe there were two things that just weren't to be had in Europe. One was a hot plate and the other was a glass of cold water. Well, the cold water one can do without; but a hot plate is more difficult. I'd got so discouraged with the cold wet ones I encountered everywhere that when I was arranging with Cook's Agency about my room here I explained to them 'I don't mind where I go to. I don't care what the expense may be. But for mercy's sake find me an hotel where I can get a hot plate by ringing for it.'"

Mother, though outwardly all sympathy, found this a little bewildering. She had a momentary vision of Mr Prodger ringing for hot plates to be brought to him at all hours. Such strange things to want in any numbers.

"I have always heard the American hotels are so very well equipped," said Miss Anderson. "Telephones in all the rooms and even tape machines."

Milly could see Miss Anderson reading that tape machine.

"I should like to go to America awfully," she cried, as Marie brought in the lamb and set it before Mother.

"There's certainly nothing wrong with America," said Mr Prodger soberly. "America's a great country. What are they? Peas? Well, I just take a few. I don't eat peas as a rule. No, no salad, thank you. Not with the hot meat."

"But what makes you want to go to America?" Miss Anderson ducked forward, smiling at Milly, and her eyeglasses fell into her plate, just escaping the gravy.

Because one wants to go everywhere, was the real answer. But Milly's flower-blue gaze rested thoughtfully on Miss Anderson as she said, "The ice-cream. I adore ice-cream."

"Do you?" said Mr Prodger, and he put down his fork; he seemed moved. "So you're fond of ice-cream, are you, Miss Fawcett?"

Milly transferred her dazzling gaze to him. It said she was.

"Well," said Mr Prodger quite playfully, and he began eating again, "I'd like to see you get it. I'm sorry we can't manage to ship some across. I like to see young people have just what they want. It seems right, somehow."

Kind man! Would he have any more lamb?

Lunch passed so pleasantly, so quickly, that the famous piece of gorgonzola was on the table in all its fatness and richness before there had been an awkward moment. The truth was that Mr Prodger proved most easy to entertain, most ready to chat. As a rule men were not fond of chat as Mother understood it. They did not seem to understand that it does not matter very much what one says; the important thing is not to let the conversation drop. Strange. Even the best of men ignored that simple rule. They refused to realise that conversation is like a dear little baby that is brought in to be handed round. You must rock it, nurse it, keep it on the move if you want it to keep on smiling. What could be simpler? But even Father . . . Mother winced away from memories that were not as sweet as memories ought to be.

All the same, she could not help hoping that Father saw what a successful little lunch party it was. He did so love to see Milly happy, and the child looked more animated than she had done for weeks. She had lost that dreamy expression, which, though very sweet, did not seem natural at her age. Perhaps what she wanted was not so much Easton's Syrup as taking out of herself.

"I have been very selfish," thought Mother, blaming herself as usual. She put her hand on Milly's arm; she pressed it gently as they rose from the table. And Marie held the door open for the white and the grey figure; for Miss Anderson, who peered short-sightedly, as though looking for something; for Mr Prodger, who brought up the rear, walking stately, with the benign air of a Monsieur who has eaten well.

IV

Beyond the balcony, the gardens, the palms and the sea lay bathed in quivering brightness. Not a leaf moved; the oranges were little worlds of burning light. There was the sound of grasshoppers ringing their tiny tambourines, and the hum of bees as they hovered, as though to taste their joy in advance, before burrowing close into the warm wide-open stocks and roses. The sound of the sea was like a breath, was like a sigh.

Did the little group on the balcony hear it? Mother's fingers moved among the black and gold coffee-cups; Miss Anderson brought the most uncomfortable chair out of the salon and sat down. Mr Prodger put his large hand on to the yellow stone ledge of the balcony and remarked gravely, "This balcony rail is just as hot as it can be."

"They say," said Mother, "that the greatest heat of the day is at about half-past two. We have certainly noticed it is very hot then."

"Yes, it's lovely then," murmured Milly, and she stretched out her hand to the sun. "It's simply baking!"

"Then you're not afraid of the sunshine?" said Mr Prodger, taking his coffee from Mother. "No, thank you. I won't take any cream. Just one lump of sugar." And he sat down balancing the little, chattering cup on his broad knee.

"No, I adore it," answered Milly, and she began to nibble the lump of sugar. . . .

Six Years After

IT WAS NOT the afternoon to be on deck — on the contrary, it was exactly the afternoon when there is no snugger place than a warm cabin, a warm bunk. Tucked up with a rug, a hot-water bottle and a piping hot cup of tea she would not have minded the weather in the least. But he — hated cabins, hated to be inside anywhere more than was absolutely necessary. He had a passion for keeping, as he called it, above board, especially when he was travelling. And it wasn't surprising, considering the enormous amount of time he spent cooped up in the office. So, when he rushed away from her as soon as they got on board and came back five minutes later to say he had secured two deck-chairs on the lee side and the steward was undoing the rugs, her voice through the high sealskin collar murmured "Good"; and because he was looking at her, she smiled with bright eyes and blinked quickly, as if to say, "Yes, perfectly all right — absolutely." And she meant it.

"Then we'd better —" said he, and he tucked her hand inside his arm and began to rush her off to where their chairs stood. But she just had time to breathe, "Not so fast, Daddy, please," when he remembered too and slowed down.

Strange! They had been married twenty-eight years, and it was still an effort to him, each time, to adapt his pace to hers.

"Not cold, are you?" he asked, glancing sideways at her. Her little nose, geranium pink above the dark fur, was answer enough. But she thrust her free hand into the velvet pocket of her jacket and murmured gaily, "I shall be glad of my rug."

He pressed her tighter to his side — a quick, nervous pressure. He knew, of course, that she ought to be down in the cabin; he knew that it was no afternoon for her to be sitting on deck, in this cold and raw mist, lee side or no lee side, rugs or no rugs, and he realised how she must be hating it. But he had come to believe that it really was easier for her to make these sacrifices than it was for him. Take their present case, for instance. If he had gone down to the cabin with her, he would have been miserable the whole time, and he couldn't have helped showing it. At any rate, she would have found him out. Whereas, having made up her mind to fall in with his ideas, he would have betted anybody she would even go so far as to enjoy the experience. Not because she was without personality of her own. Good Lord! She was absolutely brimming with it. But because . . . but here his thoughts always stopped. Here they always felt the need of a cigar, as it were. And, looking at the cigar-tip, his fine blue eyes narrowed. It was a law of marriage, he supposed. . . . All the same, he always felt guilty when he asked these sacrifices of her. That was what the quick pressure meant. His being said to her being: "You do understand, don't you?" and there was an answering tremor of her fingers, "I *understand*."

Certainly the steward — good little chap — had done all in his power to make them comfortable. He had put up their chairs in whatever warmth there was and out of the smell. She did hope he would be tipped adequately. It was on occasions like these (and her life seemed to be full of such occasions) that she wished it was the woman who controlled the purse.

"Thank you, steward. That will do beautifully."

"Why are stewards so often delicate-looking?" she wondered, as her feet were tucked under. "This poor little chap looks as though he'd got a chest, and yet one would have thought . . . the sea air . . ."

The button of the pigskin purse was undone. The tray was tilted. She saw sixpences, shillings, half-crowns.

"I should give him five shillings," she decided, "and tell him to buy himself a good nourishing —"

He was given a shilling, and he touched his cap and seemed genuinely grateful.

Well, it might have been worse. It might have been sixpence. It might, indeed. For at that moment Father turned towards her and said, half apologetically, stuffing the purse back, "I gave him a shilling. I think it was worth it, don't you?"

"Oh, quite! Every bit!" said she.

It is extraordinary how peaceful it feels on a little steamer once the bustle of leaving port is over. In a quarter of an hour one might have been at sea for days. There is something almost touching, childish, in the way people submit themselves to the new conditions. They go to bed in the early afternoon, they shut their eyes and "it's night" like little children who turn the table upside down and cover themselves with the table-cloth. And those who remain on deck — they seem to be always the same, those few hardened men travellers — pause, light their pipes, stamp softly, gaze out to sea, and their voices are subdued as they walk up and down. The long-legged little girl chases after the red-cheeked boy, but soon both are captured; and the old sailor, swinging an unlighted lantern, passes and disappears. . . .

He lay back, the rug up to his chin, and she saw he was breathing deeply. Sea air! If anyone believed in sea air it was he. He had the strongest faith in its tonic qualities. But the great thing was, according to him, to fill the lungs with it the moment you came on board. Otherwise, the sheer strength of it was enough to give you a chill. . . .

She gave a small chuckle, and he turned to her quickly. "What is it?"

"It's your cap," she said. "I never can get used to you in a cap. You look such a thorough burglar."

"Well, what the deuce am I to wear?" He shot up one grey eyebrow and wrinkled his nose. "It's a very good cap, too. Very fine specimen of its kind. It's got a very rich white satin lining." He paused. He declaimed, as he had hundreds of times before at this stage, "Rich and rare were the gems she wore."

But she was thinking he really was childishly proud of the white satin lining. He would like to have taken off his cap and made her feel it. "Feel the quality!" How often had she rubbed between finger and thumb his coat, his shirt cuff, tie, sock, linen handkerchief, while he said that.

She slipped down more deeply into her chair.

And the little steamer pressed on, pitching gently, over the grey, unbroken, gently moving water, that was veiled with slanting rain.

Far out, as though idly, listlessly, gulls were flying. Now they settled on the waves, now they beat up into the rainy air and shone against the pale sky like the lights within a pearl. They looked cold and lonely. How lonely it will be when we have passed by, she thought. There will be nothing but the waves and those birds and rain falling.

She gazed through the rust-spotted railing along which big drops trembled, until suddenly she shut her lids. It was as if a warning voice inside her head said, "Don't look!"

"No, I won't," she decided. "It's too depressing, much too depressing."

But, immediately, she opened her eyes and looked again. Lonely birds, water lifting, white pale sky — how were they changed?

And it seemed to her there was a presence far out there, between the sky and the water; someone very desolated and longing watched them pass and cried as if to stop them — but cried to her alone.

"Mother!"

"Don't leave me," sounded in the cry. "Don't forget me! You are forgetting me, you know you are!" And it was as though from her own breast there came the sound of childish weeping.

"My son — my precious child — it isn't true!"

Sh! How was it possible that she was sitting there on that quiet steamer beside Father and at the same time she was hushing and holding a little slender boy — so pale — who had just waked out of a dreadful dream?

"I dreamed I was in a wood — somewhere far away from everybody — and I was lying down and a great blackberry vine grew over me. And I called and called to you — and you wouldn't come — you wouldn't come — so I had to lie there for ever."

What a terrible dream! He had always had terrible dreams. How often, years ago, when he was small, she had made some excuse and escaped from their friends in the dining-room or the drawing-room to come to the foot of the stairs and listen. "Mother!" And when he was asleep, his dream had journeyed with her back into the circle of lamplight; it had taken its place there like a ghost. And now —

Far more often — at all times — in all places — like now, for instance — she never settled down, she was never off her guard for a moment but she heard him. He wanted her. "I am coming as fast as I can! As fast as I can!" But the dark stairs have no ending, and the worst dream of all — the one that is always the same — goes for ever and ever uncomforted.

This is anguish! How is it to be borne? Still, it is not the idea of her suffering which is unbearable — it is his. Can one do nothing for the dead? And for a long time the answer had been — Nothing!

And then finally there is his first leave. She does not go to the station to meet him. Daddy goes alone. As a matter of fact she is frightened to go. The shock may upset her and spoil their joy. So she tries to bear it at home —

Late afternoon. The lights on. Gorgeous fires everywhere — in his bedroom too, of course. She goes to see it too often, but each time there is something to be done — the curtains to be drawn — or she makes sure he has enough blankets. For some reason there is no place for the girls in this memory; they might be unborn. She is alone in that warm breathing bright house except for the servants. Each time she comes into the hall she hears that distant twitter from the kitchen, or the race of steps down the area. *They* are on the lookout. And at this point she always remembers his favourite dinner: roast chicken — asparagus — meringues — champagne. And then — Oh God help me bear this moment! There's the taxi. It's turned into the square. Is it slowing now?

"Here it is 'm."

"No, Nellie — I don't think so."

Yes — yes — it is. Courage! Be brave. It's stopping. Is that Father's glove at the window? Oh, the door is open, she is on the step. Father's voice rings out, "Here he is." And all at one and the same moment the taxi stops, and bursts open. A young muffled figure bounds up the steps.

"Mummy!"

"My precious, precious son!"

But here it's no use. Here she must break down. Just a moment — just one. Pressing her head against the cold buttons of his British warm.

"Child!"

He holds her. And his father is behind him grabbing his shoulder, and his laugh rings out —

"Well, you've got him. Are you satisfied?"

The door is shut. He is pulling off his gloves, and scarf and coat, and pressing them on to the chest in the hall. The old familiar quick shot back of his head while he looks at her, laughing, while he describes how he spotted Daddy immediately — and Father absolutely refused to recognise *him*.

. . . But softly without a sound the dark curtain has rolled down. There is no more to come. That is the end of the play. But it can't end like that — so suddenly. There must be more. No, it's cold, it's still. There is nothing to be gained by waiting.

But — did he go back again? Or, when the war was over, did he come home for good? Surely, he will marry — later on — not for several years. Surely, one day I shall remember his wedding and my first grandchild — a beautiful dark-haired boy born in the early morning — a lovely morning — spring!

"Oh, Mother, it's not fair to me to put these ideas into my head! Stop, Mother, stop! When I think of all I have missed, I can't bear it."

"I can't bear it!" She sits up breathing the words and tosses the dark rug away. It is colder than ever, and now the dusk is falling, falling like ash upon the pallid water.

And the little steamer, growing determined, throbbed on, pressed on, as if at the end of the journey there waited . . .

Daphne

I HAD BEEN IN Port Willin six months when I decided to give a one-man show Not that I was particularly keen, but little Field, the picture-shop man, had just started a gallery and he wanted me — begged me, rather — to kick off for him. He was a decent little chap; I hadn't the heart to refuse. And besides, as it happened, I had a good deal of stuff that I felt it would be rather fun to palm off on any one who was fool enough to buy it. So with these high aims I had the cards printed, the pictures framed in plain white frames, and God knows how many cups and saucers ordered for the Private View.

What was I doing in Port Willin? Oh well — why not? I'll own it does sound an unlikely spot, but when you are an impermanent movable, as I am, it's just those unlikely spots that have a trick of holding you. I arrived, intending to stay a week and go on to Fiji. But I had letters to one or two people, and the morning of my arrival, hanging over the side of the ship while we were waiting in the stream, with nothing on earth to do but stare, I took an extra-ordinary fancy to the shape — to the look of the place.

It's a small town, you know, planted at the edge of a fine deep harbour like a lake. Behind it, on either side, there are hills. The houses are built of light painted wood. They have iron roofs coloured red. And there are big dark plumy trees massed together, breaking up those light shapes, giving a depth — warmth — making a composition of it well worth looking at. . . . Well, we needn't go into that — But it had me that fine morning. And the first days after my arrival, walking, or driving out in one of the big swinging, rocking cabs, I took an equal fancy to the people.

Not to quite all of them. The men left me cold. Yes, I must say, colonial men are not the brightest specimens. But I never struck a place where the average of female attractiveness was so high. You can't help noticing it, for a peculiarity of Port Willin is the number of its teashops and the vast quantity of tea absorbed by its inhabit-ants. Not tea only — sandwiches, cream cakes, ices, fruit salad with fresh pineapples. From eleven o'clock in the morning you meet with couples and groups of girls and young married women hurrying off to their first tea. It was a real eleven o'clock function. Even the business men knocked off and went to a café. And the same thing happened in the afternoon. From four until half-past six the streets were gay as a garden. Which reminds me, it was early spring when I arrived and the town smelled of moist earth and the first flowers. In fact, wherever one went one got a strong whiff, like the whiff of violets in a wood, which was enough in itself to make one feel like lingering. . . .

There was a theatre too, a big bare building plastered over with red and blue bills which gave it an oriental look in that blue air, and a touring company was playing "San Toy". I went my first evening. I found it, for some reason, fearfully exciting. The inside smelled of gas, of glue and burnt paper. Whistling draughts cut along the corridors — a strong wind among the orchestra kept the palms trembling, and now and again the curtain blew out and there was a glimpse of a pair of large feet walking rapidly away. But what women! What girls in muslin dressed with velvet sashes and little caps edged with swansdown! In the intervals long ripples of laughter sounded from the stalls, from the dress-circle. And I leaned against a pillar that looked as though it was made of wedding-cake icing — and fell in love with whole rows at a time. . . .

Then I presented my letters, I was asked out to dine, and I met these charmers in their own homes. That decided it. They were something I had never known before — so gay, so friendly, so impressed with the idea of one's being an artist! It was rather like finding oneself in the playground of an extremely attractive girls' school.

I painted the Premier's daughter, a dark beauty, against a tree hung with long, bell-like flowers as white as wax. I painted a girl with a pigtail curled up on a white sofa playing with a pale-red fan . . . and a little blonde in a black jacket with pearl grey gloves. . . . I painted like fury.

I'm fond of women. As a matter of fact I'm a great deal more at my ease with women than I am with men. Because I've cultivated them, I suppose. You see, it's like this with me. I've always had enough money to live on, and the consequence is I have never had to mix with people more than I wished. And I've equally always had — well, I suppose you might call it — a passion for painting. Painting is far and away the most important thing in life — as I see it. But — my work's my own affair. It's the separate compartment which is me. No strangers allowed in. I haven't the smallest desire to explain what it is I'm after — or to hear other men. If people like my work I'm pleased. If they don't — well, if I was a shrugging person, I'd shrug. This sounds arrogant. It isn't; I know my limit-ations. But the truth about oneself always sounds arrogant, as no doubt you've observed.

But women — well, I can only speak for myself — I find the pres-ence of women, the consciousness of women, an absolute neces-sity. I know they are considered a distraction, that the very Big Pots seal themselves in their hives to keep away. All I can say is work without women would be to me like dancing without music or food without wine or a sailing boat without a breeze. They just give me that . . . what is it? Stimulus is not enough; inspiration is far too much. That — well, if I knew what it is, I should have solved a bigger problem than my own! And problems aren't in my line.

I expected a mob at my Private View, and I got it, too. . . . What I hadn't reckoned on was that there would be no men. It was one thing to ask a painter fellow to knock you up something to the tune of fifty guineas or so, but it was quite another to make an ass of yourself staring. The Port Willin men would as soon have gazed into shops. True, when you came to Europe, you visited the galleries, but then you shop-gazed too. It didn't matter what you did in Europe. You could walk about for a week without being recognised.

So there were little Field and I absolutely alone among all that loveliness; it frightened him out of his life, but I didn't mind, I thought it rather fun, especially as the sightseers didn't hesitate to find my pictures amusing. I'm by no means an out-and-out modern, as they say; people like violins and landscapes of telegraph poles leave me cold. But Port Willin is still trying to swallow Rossetti, and Hope by Watts is looked upon as very advanced. It was natural my pictures should surprise them. The fat old Lady Mayoress became quite hysterical. She drew me over to one drawing; she patted my arm with her fan.

"I don't wonder you drew her slipping out," she gurgled. "And how depressed she looks! The poor dear never could have sat down in it. It's much too small. There ought to be a little cake of Pears' Soap on the floor." And overcome by her own joke, she flopped on the little double bench that ran down the middle of the room, and even her fan seemed to laugh.

At that moment two girls passed in front of us. One I knew, a big fair girl called May Pollock, pulled her companion by the sleeve. "Daphne!" she said. "Daphne!" And the other turned towards her, then towards us, smiled and was born, christened part of my world from that moment.

"Daphne!" Her quick, beautiful smile answered. . . .

Saturday morning was gloriously fine. When I woke up and saw the sun streaming over the polished floor I felt like a little boy who has been promised a picnic. It was all I could do not to telephone Daphne. Was she feeling the same? It seemed somehow such a terrific lark that we should be going off together like this, just with a couple of rucksacks and our bathing suits. I thought of other week-ends, the preparation, the emotional tension, the amount of managing they'd needed. But I couldn't really think of them; I couldn't be bothered, they belonged to another life. . . .

It seemed to me suddenly so preposterous that two people should be as happy as we were and not be happier. Here we were, alone, miles away from everybody, free as air, and in love with each other. I looked again at Daphne, at her slender shoulders, her throat, her bosom, and, passionately in love, I decided, with fervour: Wouldn't it be rather absurd, then, to behave like a couple of children? Wouldn't she even, in spite of all she had said, be disappointed if we did? . . .

And I went off at a tremendous pace, not because I thought she'd run after me, but I did think she might call, or I might look round.

It was one of those still, hushed days when the sea and the sky seem to melt into one another, and it is long before the moisture dies on the leaves and grasses. One of those days when the sea smells strong and there are gulls standing in a row on the sand. The smoke from our wood fire hung in the air and the smoke of my pipe mingled with it. I caught myself staring at nothing. I felt dull and angry. I couldn't get over the ridiculous affair. You see, my *amour propre* was wounded.

Monday morning was grey, cloudy, one of those mornings peculiar to the seaside when everything, the sea most of all, seems exhausted and sullen. There had been a very high tide, the road was wet — on the beach there stood a long line of sickly-looking gulls. . . .

When we got on board she sat down on one of the green benches and, muttering something about a pipe, I walked quickly away. It was intolerable that we should still be together after what had happened. It was indecent. I only asked — I only longed for one thing — to be free of this still, unsmiling and pitiful — that was the worst of it — creature who had been my playful Daphne.

For answer I telephoned her at once and asked if I might come and see her that evening. Her voice sounded grave, unlike the voice I remembered, and she seemed to deliberate. There was a long pause before she said, "Yes — perhaps that would be best."

"Then I shall come at half-past six."

"Very well."

And we went into a room full of flowers and very large art photographs of the Harbour by Night, A Misty Day, Moonrise over the Water, and I know I wondered if she admired them.

"Why did you send me that letter?"

"Oh, but I had to," said Daphne. "I meant every word of it. I only let you come to-night to . . . No, I know I shall disappoint you. I'm wiser than you are for all your experience. I shan't be able to live up to it. I'm not the person for you. Really I'm not!" . . .

Father and the Girls

I

AT MIDDAY, Ernestine, who had come down from the mountains with her mother to work in the vineyards belonging to the hotel, heard the faint, far-away *chuff-chuff* of the train from Italy. Trains were a novelty to Ernestine; they were fascinating, unknown, terrible. What were they like as they came tearing their way through the valley, plunging between the mountains as if not even the mountains could stop them? When she saw the dark, flat breast of the engine, so bare, so powerful, hurled as it were towards her, she felt a weakness — she could have sunk to the earth. And yet she must look. So she straightened up, stopped pulling at the blue-green leaves, tugging at the long, bright-green, curly suckers, and, with eyes like a bird, stared. The vines were very tall. There was nothing to be seen of Ernestine but her beautiful, youthful bosom buttoned into a blue cotton jacket and her small, dark head covered with a faded cherry-coloured handkerchief.

Chiff-chuff-chaff. Chiff-chuff-chaff, sounded the train. Now a wisp of white smoke shone and melted. Now there was another, and the monster itself came into sight and snorting horribly drew up at a little, toy-like station five minutes away. The railway ran at the bottom of the hotel garden which was perched high and surrounded by a stone wall. Steps cut in the stone led to the terraces where the vines were planted. Ernestine, looking out from the leaves like a bright bird, saw the terrible engine and looked beyond it at doors swinging open, at strangers stepping down. She would never know who they were or where they had come from. A moment ago they were not here; perhaps by to-morrow they would be gone again. And looking like a bird herself, she remembered how, at home, in the late autumn, she had sometimes seen strange birds in the fir tree that were there one day and gone the next. Where from? Where to? She felt an ache in her bosom. Wings were tight-folded there. Why could she not stretch them out and fly away and away? . . .

From the first-class carriage tall, thin Emily alighted and gave her hand to Father whose brittle legs seemed to wave in the air as they felt for the iron step. Taller, thinner Edith followed, carrying Father's light overcoat, his field-glasses on a strap and his new Baedeker. The blond hotel porter came forward. Wasn't that nice? He could speak as good English as you or me. So Edith had no trouble at all in explaining how, as they were going on by the morning train to-morrow, they would only need their suit-cases and what was left in the compartment. Was there a carriage outside? Yes, a carriage was there. But if they cared to walk there was a private entrance through the hotel gardens. . . . No, they wouldn't walk.

"You wouldn't care to walk, would you, Father dear?"

"No, Edith, I won't walk. Do you girls wanna walk?"

"Why no, Father, not without you, dear."

And the blond hotel porter leading, they passed through the little knot of sturdy peasants at the station gate to where the carriage waited under a group of limes.

"Did you ever see anything as big as that horse, Edith!" cried Emily. She was always the first to exclaim about things.

"It is a very big horse," sang Edith, more sober. "It's a farm horse, from the look of it, and it's been working. See how hot it is." Edith had so much observation. The big, brown horse, his sides streaked with dark sweat, tossed his head and the bells on his collar set up a loud jangling.

"Hu-yup!" called the young peasant driver warningly, from his seat on the high box.

Father, who was just about to get in, drew back, a little scared.

"You don't think that horse will run away with us, do you, Edith?" he quavered.

"Why no, Father dear," coaxed Edith. "That horse is just as tame as you or me." So in they got, the three of them. And as the horse bounded forward his ears seemed to twitch in surprise at his friend the driver. Call that a load? Father and the girls weighed nothing. They might have been three bones, three broomsticks, three umbrellas bouncing up and down on the hard seats of the carriage. It was a mercy the hotel was so close. Father could never have stood that for more than a minute, especially at the end of a journey. Even as it was his face was quite green when Emily helped him out, straightened him, and gave him a little pull.

"It's shaken you, dear, hasn't it?" she said tenderly.

But he refused her arm into the hotel. That would create a wrong impression.

"No, no, Emily. I'm all right," said Father, as staggering a little he followed them through big glass doors into a hall as dim as a church and as chill and as deserted.

My! Wasn't that hall cold! The cold seemed to come leaping at them from the floor. It clasped the peaked knees of Edith and Emily; it leapt high as the fluttering heart of Father. For a moment they hesitated, drew together, almost gasped. But then out from the Bureau a cheerful young person, her smiling face spotted with mosquito bites, ran to meet them, and welcomed them with such real enthusiasm (in English too) that the chill first moment was forgotten.

"Aw-yes. Aw-yes. I can let you ave very naice rooms on de firs floor wid a lif. Two rooms and bart and dressing-room for de chentleman. Beautiful rooms wid sun but nort too hot. Very naice. Till tomorrow. I taike you. If you please. It is dis way. You are tired wid the churney? Launch is at half-pas tvelf. Hort worter? Aw-yes. It is wid de bart. If you please."

Father and the girls were drawn by her cheerful smiles and becks and nods along a cloister-like corridor, into the lift and up, until she flung open a heavy, dark door and stood aside for them to enter.

"It is a suite," she explained. "Wid a hall and tree doors."

Quickly she opened them. "Now I gaw to see when your luggage is gum."

And she went.

"Well!" cried Emily.

Edith stared.

Father craned his thin, old neck, looking, too.

"Did you — ever see the like, Edith?" cried Emily, in a little rush.

And Edith softly clasped her hands. Softly she sang "No, I never did, Emily. I've never seen anything just like this before."

"Sims to me a nice room," quavered Father, still hovering. "Do you girls wanna change it?"

Change it! "Why, Father dear, it's just the loveliest thing we've ever set eyes on, isn't it Emily? Sit down, Father dear, sit down in the arm-chair."

Father's pale claws gripped the velvet arms. He lowered himself; he sank with an old man's quick sigh.

Edith still stood, as if bewitched, at the door. But Emily ran over to the window and leaned out, quite girlish. . . .

For a long time now — for how long? — for countless ages — Father and the girls had been on the wing. Nice, Montreux, Biarritz, Naples, Menton, Lake Maggiore, they had seen them all and many, many more. And still they beat on, beat on, flying as if unwearied, never stopping anywhere for long. But the truth was — Oh, better not inquire what the truth was. Better not ask what it was that kept them going. Or why the only word that daunted Father was the word — home. . . .

Home! To sit around, doing nothing, listening to the clock, counting up the years, thinking back . . . thinking! To stay fixed in one place as if waiting for something or somebody. No! no! Better far to be blown over the earth like the husk, like the withered pod that the wind carries and drops and bears aloft again.

"Are you ready, girls?"

"Yes, Father dear."

"Then we'd better be off if we're to make that train."

But oh, it was a weariness, it was an unspeakable weariness. Father made no secret of his age; he was eighty-four. As for Edith and Emily — well, he looked now like their elder brother. An old, old brother and two ancient sisters, so the lovely room might have summed them up. But its shaded brightness, its beauty, the flutter of leaves at the creamy stone windows seemed only to whisper "Rest! Stay!"

Edith looked at the pale, green-panelled walls, at the doors that had lozenges and squares of green picked out in gold. She made the amazing discovery that the floor had the same pattern in wood that was traced on the high, painted ceiling. But the colour of the shining floor was marvellous; it was like tortoiseshell. In one corner there was a huge, tilted stove, milky white and blue. The low wooden bed, with its cover of quilted yellow satin, had sheaves of corn carved on the bed-posts. It looked to fanciful, tired Edith — yes — that bed looked as if it were breathing, softly, gently breathing. Outside the narrow, deep-set windows, beyond their wreaths of green, she could see a whole, tiny landscape bright as a jewel in the summer heat.

"Rest! Stay!" Was it the sound of the leaves outside? No, it was in the air; it was the room itself that whispered joyfully, shyly. Edith felt so strange that she could keep quiet no longer.

"This is a very old room, Emily," she warbled softly. "I know what it is. This hotel has not always been a hotel. It's been an old château. I feel as sure of that as that I'm standing here." Perhaps she wanted to convince herself that she was standing there. "Do you see that stove?" She walked over to the stove. "It's got figures on it. Emily," she warbled faintly, "it's 1623."

"Isn't that too wonderful!" cried Emily.

Even Father was deeply moved.

"1623? Nearly three hundred years old." And suddenly, in spite of his tiredness, he gave a thin airy, old man's chuckle. "Makes yer feel quite a chicken, don't it?" said Father.

Emily's breathless little laugh answered him; it, too, was gay.

"I'm going to see what's behind that door," she cried. And half running to the door in the middle wall she lifted the slender steel catch. It led into a larger room, into Edith's and her bedroom. But the walls were the same and the floor, and there were the same deep-set windows. Only two beds instead of one stood side by side with blue silk quilts instead of yellow. And what a beautiful old chest there was under the windows!

"Oh," cried Emily, in rapture. "Isn't it all too perfectly historical for words, Edith! It makes me feel —" She stopped, she looked at Edith who had followed her and whose thin shadow lay on the sunny floor. "Queer!" said Emily, trying to put all she felt into that one word. "I don't know what it is."

Perhaps if Edith, the discoverer, had had time she might have satisfied Emily. But a knock sounded at the outer door; it was the luggage boy. And while he brought in their suit-cases there came from downstairs the ringing of the luncheon bell. Father mustn't be kept waiting. Once a bell had gone he liked to follow it up right then. So without even a glance at the mirror — they had reached the age when it is as natural to avoid mirrors as it is to peer into them when one is young — Edith and Emily were ready.

"Are you ready, girls?"

"Yes, Father dear."

And off they went again, to the left, to the right, down a stone staircase with a broad, worn balustrade, to the left again, finding their way as if by instinct — Edith first, then Father, and Emily close behind.

But when they reached the *salle à manger*, which was as big as a ballroom, it was still empty. All gay, all glittering, the long French windows open on to the green and gold garden, the *salle à manger* stretched before them. And the fifty little tables with the fifty pots of dahlias looked as if they might begin dancing with . . .

All Serene!

AT BREAKFAST THAT MORNING they were in wonderfully good spirits. Who was responsible — he or she? It was true she made a point of looking her best in the morning; she thought it part of her duty to him — to their love, even, to wear charming little caps, funny little coats, coloured mules at breakfast time, and to see that the table was perfect as he and she — fastidious pair! — understood the word. But he, too, so fresh, well groomed and content, contributed his share. . . . She had been down first, sitting at her place when he came in. He leaned over the back of her chair, his hands on her shoulders; he bent down and lightly rubbed his cheek against hers, murmuring gently but with just enough pride of proprietorship to make her flush with delight, "Give me my tea, love." And she lifted the silver teapot that had a silver pear modelled on the lid and gave him his tea.

"Thanks. . . . You know you look awfully well this morning!"

"Do I?"

"Yes. Do that again. Look at me again. It's your eyes. They're like a child's. I've never known anyone have such shining eyes as you."

"Oh, dear!" She sighed for joy. "I do love having sweet things said to me!"

"Yes, you do — spoilt child! Shall I give you some of this?"

"No, thank you. . . . Darling!" Her hand flew across the table and clasped his hand.

"Yes?"

But she said nothing, only "Darling!" again. There was the look on his face she loved — a kind of sweet jesting. He was pretending he didn't know what she meant, and yet of course he did know. He was pretending to be feeling "Here she is — trust a woman — all ready for a passionate love scene over the breakfast table at nine o'clock in the morning." But she wasn't deceived. She knew he felt just the same as she did. That amused tolerance, that mock despair was part of the ways of men — no more.

"May I be allowed to *use* this knife please, or to put it down?"

Really! Mona had never yet got accustomed to her husband's smile. They had been married for three years. She was in love with him for countless reasons, but apart from them all, a special reason all to itself, was because of his smile. If it hadn't sounded nonsense she would have said she fell in love at first sight over and over again when he smiled. Other people felt the charm of it, too. Other women, she was certain. Sometimes she thought that even the servants watched for it. . . .

"Don't forget we're going to the theatre tonight."

"Oh, good egg! I had forgotten. It's ages since we went to a show."

"Yes, isn't it? I feel quite thrilled."

"Don't you think we might have a tiny small celebration at dinner?" ("Tiny small" was one of her expressions. But why did it sound so sweet when he used it?)

"Yes, let's. You mean champagne?" And she looked into the distance, and said in a far-away voice: "Then I must revise the sweet."

At that moment the maid came in with the letters. There were four for him, three for her. No, one of hers belonged to him, too, rather a grimy little envelope with a dab of sealing-wax on the back.

"Why do you get all the letters?" she wailed, handing it across. "It's awfully unfair. I love letters and I never get any."

"Well, I do like that!" said he. "How can you sit there and tell such awful bangers? It's the rarest thing on earth for me to get a letter in the morning. It's always you who get those mysterious epistles from girls you were at college with or faded aunts. Here, have half my pear — it's a beauty." She held out her plate.

The Rutherfords never shared their letters. It was her idea that they should not. He had been violently opposed to it at first. She couldn't help laughing; he had so absolutely misunderstood her reason.

"Good God! my dear. You're perfectly welcome to open any letters of mine that come to the house — or to read any letters of mine that may be lying about. I think I can promise you . . ."

"Oh no, no, darling, that's not what I mean. I don't suspect you." And she put her hands on his cheeks and kissed him quickly. He looked like an offended boy. "But so many of Mother's old friends write to me — confide in me — don't you know? — tell me things they wouldn't for the world tell a man. I feel it wouldn't be fair to them. Don't you see?"

He gave way at last. But "I'm old-fashioned," he said, and his smile was a little rueful. "I like to feel my wife reads my letters."

"My precious dear! I've made you unhappy." She felt so repentant; she didn't know quite about what. "Of course I'd love to read . . ."

"No, no! That's all right. It's understood. We'll keep the bond." And they had kept it.

He slit open the grimy envelope. He began to read. "Damn!" he said and thrust out his under lip.

"Why, what is it? Something horrid?"

"No — annoying. I shall be late this evening. A man wants to meet me at the office at six o'clock."

"Was that a business letter?" She sounded surprised.

"Yes, why?"

"It looked so awfully unbusinesslike. The sealing-wax and the funny writing — much more like a woman's than a man's."

He laughed. He folded the letter, put it in his pocket and picked up the envelope. "Yes," he said, "it is queer, isn't it. I shouldn't have noticed. How quick you are! But it does look exactly like a woman's hand. That capital R, for instance" — he flipped the envelope across to her.

"Yes, and that squiggle underneath. I should have said a rather uneducated female . . ."

"As a matter of fact," said Hugh, "he's a mining engineer." And he got up, began to stretch and then stopped. "I say, what a glorious morning! Why do I have to go to the office instead of staying at home and playing with you?" And he came over to her and locked his arms round her neck. "Tell me that, little lovely one."

"Oh," she leaned against him, "I wish you could. Life's arranged badly for people like you and me. And now you're going to be late this evening."

"Never mind," said he. "All the rest of the time's ours. Every single bit of it. We shan't come back from the theatre to find —"

"Our porch black with mining engineers." She laughed. Did other people — could other people — was it possible that anyone before had ever loved as they loved? She squeezed her head against him — she heard his watch ticking — precious watch!

"What are those purple floppy flowers in my bedroom?" he murmured.

"Petunias."

"You smell exactly like a petunia."

And he raised her up. She drew towards him. "Kiss me," said he.

II

It was her habit to sit on the bottom stair and watch his final preparations. Strange it should be so fascinating to see someone brush his hat, choose a pair of gloves and give a last quick look in the round mirror. But it was the same when he was shaving. Then she loved to curl up on the hard little couch in his dressing-room; she was so absorbed, as intent as he. How fantastic he looked, like a pierrot, like a mask, with those dark eyebrows, liquid eyes and the brush of fresh colour on his cheek-bones above the lather! But that was not her chief feeling. No, it was what she felt on the stairs, too. It was, "So this is my husband, so this is the man I've married, this is the stranger who walked across the lawn that afternoon swinging his tennis racket and bowed, rolling up his shirt-sleeves. This is not only my lover and my husband but my brother, my dearest friend, my playmate, even at times a kind of very perfect father too. And here is where we live. Here is his room — and here is our hall." She seemed to be showing their house and him to her other self, the self she had been before she had met him. Deeply admiring, almost awed by so much happiness, that other self looked on. . . .

"Will I do?" He stood there smiling, stroking on his gloves. But although he wouldn't like her to say the things she often longed to say about his appearance, she did think she detected that morning just the very faintest boyish showing-off. Children who know they are admired look like that at their mother.

"Yes, you'll do. . . ." Perhaps at that moment she was proud of him as a mother is proud; she could have blessed him before he went his way. Instead she stood in the porch thinking, "There he goes. The man I've married. The stranger who came across the lawn." The fact was never less wonderful. . . .

It was never less wonderful, never. It was even more wonderful if anything, and the reason was — Mona ran back into the house, into the drawing-room and sat down to the piano. Oh, why bother about reasons — She began to sing,

> See, love, I bring thee flowers
> To charm thy pain!

But joy — joy breathless and exulting thrilled in her voice, on the word "pain" her lips parted in such a happy — dreadfully unsympathetic smile that she felt quite ashamed. She stopped playing, she turned round on the piano stool facing the room. How different it looked in the morning, how severe and remote. The grey chairs with the fuchsia-coloured cushions, the black and gold carpet, the bright green silk curtains might have belonged to anybody. It was like a stage setting with the curtain still down. She had no right to be there, and as she thought that a queer little chill caught her; it seemed so extraordinary that anything, even a chair, should turn away from, should not respond to her happiness.

"I don't like this room in the morning, I don't like it at all," she decided, and she ran upstairs to finish dressing. Ran into their big, shadowy bedroom . . . and leaned over the starry petunias. . . .

A Bad Idea

SOMETHING'S HAPPENED TO ME — something bad. And I don't know what to do about it. I don't see any way out for the life of me. The worst of it is, I can't get this thing into focus — if you know what I mean. I just feel in a muddle — in the hell of a muddle. It ought to be plain to anyone that I'm not the kind of man to get mixed up in a thing like this. I'm not one of your actor Johnnies, or a chap in a book. I'm — well, I knew what I was all right until yesterday. But now — I feel helpless, yes, that's the word, helpless. Here I sit, chucking stones at the sea like a child that's missed its mother. And everybody else has cut along home hours ago and tea's over and it's getting on for time to light the lamp. I shall have to go home too, sooner or later. I see that, of course. In fact, would you believe it? at this very moment I wish I was there in spite of everything. What's she doing? My wife, I mean. Has she cleared away? Or has she stayed there staring at the table with the plates pushed back? My God! when I think that I could howl like a dog — if you know what I mean. . . .

I should have realised it was all U.P. this morning when she didn't get up for breakfast. I did, in a way. But I couldn't face it. I had the feeling that if I said nothing special and just treated it as one of her bad headache days and went off to the office, by the time I got back this evening the whole affair would have blown over somehow. No, that wasn't it. I felt a bit like I do now, "helpless". What was I to do? Just go on. That was all I could think of. So I took her up a cup of tea and a couple of slices of thin bread and butter as per usual on her headache days. The blind was still down. She was lying on her back. I think she had a wet handkerchief on her forehead. I'm not sure, for I couldn't look at her. It was a beastly feeling. And she said in a weak kind of voice, "Put the jug on the table, will you?" I put it down. I said, "Can I do anything?" And she said, "No. I'll be all right in half an hour." But her voice, you know! It did for me. I barged out as quick as I could, snatched my hat and stick from the hall-stand and dashed off for the tram.

Here's a queer thing — you needn't believe me if you don't want to — the moment I got out of the house I forgot that about my wife. It was a splendid morning, soft, with the sun making silver ducks on the sea. The kind of morning when you know it's going to keep hot and fine all day. Even the tram bell sounded different, and the little school kids crammed between people's knees had bunches of flowers. I don't know — I can't understand why — I just felt happy, but happy in a way I'd never been before, happy to beat the band! That wind that had been so strong the night before was still blowing a bit. It felt like her — the other — touching me. Yes it did. Brought it back, every bit of it. If I told you how it took me, you'd say I was mad. I felt reckless — didn't care if I was late for the office or not and I wanted to do every one a kindness. I helped the little kids out of the tram. One little chap dropped his cap, and when I picked it up for him and said, "Here, sonny!" . . . well, it was all I could do not to make a fool of myself.

At the office it was just the same. It seemed to me I'd never known the fellows at the office before. When old Fisher came over to my desk and put down a couple of giant sweet peas as per usual with his "Beat 'em, old man, beat 'em!" — I didn't feel annoyed. I didn't care that he was riddled with conceit about his garden. I just looked at them and I said quietly, "Yes, you've done it this time." He didn't know what to make of it. Came back in about five minutes and asked me if I had a headache.

And so it went on all day. In the evening I dashed home with the home-going crowd, pushed open the gate, saw the hall-door open as it always is and sat down on the little chair just inside to take off my boots. My slippers were there, of course. This seemed to me a good sign. I put my boots into the rack in the cupboard under the stairs, changed my office coat and made for the kitchen. I knew my wife was there. Wait a bit. The only thing I couldn't manage was my whistling as per usual, "I often lie awake and think, What a dreadful thing is work. . . ." I had a try, but nothing came of it. Well, I opened the kitchen door and said, "Hullo! How's everybody?" But as soon as I'd said that — even before — I knew the worst had happened. She was standing at the table beating the salad dressing. And when she looked up and gave a kind of smile and said "Hullo!" you could have knocked me down! My wife looked dreadful — there's no other word for it. She must have been crying all day. She'd put some white flour stuff on her face to take away the marks — but it only made her look worse. She must have seen I spotted something, for she caught up the cup of cream and poured some into the salad bowl — like she always does, you know, so quick, so neat, in her own way — and began beating again. I said, "Is your head better?" But she didn't seem to hear. She said, "Are you going to water the garden before or after supper?" What could I say? I said, "After," and went off to the dining-room, opened the evening paper and sat by the open window — well, hiding behind that paper, I suppose.

I shall never forget sitting there. People passing by, going down the road, sounded so peaceful. And a man passed with some cows. I — I envied him. My wife came in and out. Then she called me to supper and we sat down. I suppose we ate some cold meat and salad. I don't remember. We must have. But neither of us spoke. It's like a dream now. Then she got up, changed the plates, and went to the larder for the pudding. Do you know what the pudding was? Well, of course, it wouldn't mean anything to you. It was my favourite — the kind she only made me on special occasions — honeycomb cream. . . .

A Man and His Dog

TO LOOK AT MR POTTS one would have thought that there at least went someone who had nothing to boast about. He was a little, insignificant fellow with a crooked tie, a hat too small for him and a coat too large. The brown canvas portfolio that he carried to and from the Post Office every day was not like a business man's portfolio. It was like a child's school satchel; it did up even with a round-eyed button. One imagined there were crumbs and an apple core inside. And then there was something funny about his boots, wasn't there? Through the laces his coloured socks peeped out. What the dickens had the chap done with the tongues? "Fried 'em," suggested the wit of the Chesney bus. Poor old Potts! "More likely buried 'em in his garden." Under his arm he clasped an umbrella. And in wet weather when he put it up he disappeared completely. He was not. He was a walking umbrella — no more — the umbrella became his shell.

Mr Potts lived in a little bungalow on Chesney Flat. The bulge of the water tank to one side gave it a mournful air, like a little bungalow with the toothache. There was no garden. A path had been cut in the paddock turf from the gate to the front door, and two beds, one round, one oblong, had been cut in what was going to be the front lawn. Down that path went Potts every morning at half-past eight and was picked up by the Chesney bus; up that path walked Potts every evening while the great kettle of a bus droned on. In the late evening, when he crept as far as the gate, eager to smoke a pipe — he wasn't allowed to smoke any nearer to the house than that — so humble, so modest was his air, that the big, merrily shining stars seemed to wink at each other, to laugh, to say, "Look at him! Let's throw something!"

When Potts got out of the tram at the Fire Station to change into the Chesney bus he saw that something was up. The car was there all right, but the driver was off his perch; he was flat on his face half under the engine, and the conductor, his cap off, sat on a step rolling a cigarette and looking dreamy. A little group of business men and a woman clerk or two stood staring at the empty car; there was something mournful, pitiful about the way it leaned to one side and shivered faintly when the driver shook something. It was like someone who'd had an accident and tries to say: "Don't touch me! Don't come near me! Don't hurt me!"

But all this was so familiar — the cars had only been running to Chesney the last few months — that nobody said anything, nobody asked anything. They just waited on the off chance. In fact, two or three decided to walk it as Potts came up. But Potts didn't want to walk unless he had to. He was tired. He'd been up half the night rubbing his wife's chest — she had one of her mysterious pains — and helping the sleepy servant girl heat compresses and hot-water bottles and make tea. The window was blue and the roosters had started crowing before he lay down finally with feet like ice. And all this was familiar, too.

Standing at the edge of the pavement and now and again changing his brown canvas portfolio from one hand to the other Potts began to live over the night before. But it was vague, shadowy. He saw himself moving like a crab, down the passage to the cold kitchen and back again. The two candles quivered on the dark chest of drawers, and as he bent over his wife her big eyes suddenly flashed and she cried:

"I get no sympathy — no sympathy. You only do it because you have to. Don't contradict me. I can see you grudge doing it."

Trying to soothe her only made matters worse. There had been an awful scene ending with her sitting up and saying solemnly with her hand raised: "Never mind, it will not be for long now." But the sound of these words frightened her so terribly that she flung back on the pillow and sobbed, "Robert! Robert!" Robert was the name of the young man to whom she had been engaged years ago, before she met Potts. And Potts was very glad to hear him invoked. He had come to know that meant the crisis was over and she'd begin to quieten down. . . .

By this time Potts had wheeled round; he had walked across the pavement to the paling fence that ran beside. A piece of light grass pushed through the fence and some slender silky daisies. Suddenly he saw a bee alight on one of the daisies and the flower leaned over, swayed, shook, while the little bee clung and rocked. And as it flew away the petals fluttered as if joyfully. . . . Just for an instant Potts dropped into the world where this happened. He brought from it the timid smile with which he walked back to the car. But now everybody had disappeared except one young girl who stood beside the empty car reading.

At the tail of the procession came Potts in a cassock so much too large for him that it looked like a night-shirt and you felt that he ought to be carrying not a hymn and a prayer book but a candle. His voice was a very light plaintive tenor. It surprised everybody. It seemed to surprise him, too. But it was so plaintive that when he cried "for the wings, for the wings of a dove", the ladies in the congregation wanted to club together and buy him a pair.

Lino's nose quivered so pitifully, there was such a wistful, timid look in his eyes, that Potts' heart was wrung. But, of course, he would not show it. "Well," he said sternly, "I suppose you'd better come home." And he got up off the bench. Lino got up, too, but stood still, holding up a paw.

"But there's one thing," said Potts, turning and facing him squarely, "that we'd better be clear about before you do come. And it's this." He pointed his finger at Lino, who started as though he expected to be shot. But he kept his bewildered wistful eyes upon his master. "Stop this pretence of being a fighting dog," said Potts more sternly than ever. "You're not a fighting dog. You're a watch dog. That's what you are. Very well. Stick to it. But it's this infernal boasting I can't stand. It's that that gets me."

In the moment's pause that followed while Lino and his master looked at each other it was curious how strong a resemblance was between them. Then Potts turned again and made for home.

And timidly, as though falling over his own paws, Lino followed after the humble little figure of his master. . . .

Such a Sweet Old Lady

WHY DID OLD MRS TRAVERS wake so early nowadays? She would like to have slept for another three hours at least. But no, every morning at almost precisely the same time, at half past four, she was wide awake. For — nowadays, again — she woke always in the same way, with a slight start, a small shock, lifting her head from the pillow with a quick glance as if she fancied someone had called her, or as if she were trying to remember for certain whether this was the same wall-paper, the same window she had seen last night before Warner switched off the light. . . . Then the small, silvery head pressed the white pillow again, and just for a moment, before the agony of lying awake began, old Mrs Travers was happy. Her heart quietened down, she breathed deeply, she even smiled. Yet once more the tide of darkness had risen, had floated her, had carried her away; and once more it had ebbed, it had withdrawn, casting her up where it had found her, shut in by the same wall-paper, stared at by the same window — still safe — still *there!*

Now the church clock sounded from outside, slow, languid, faint, as if it chimed the half-hour in its sleep. She felt under the pillow for her watch; yes, it said the same: half-past four. Three and a half hours before Warner came in with her tea. Oh dear, would she be able to stand it? She moved her legs restlessly. And, staring at the prim, severe face of the watch, it seemed to her that the hands — the minute hand especially — knew that she was watching them and held back — just a very little — on purpose. . . . Very strange, she had never got over the feeling that watch hated her. It had been Henry's. Twenty years ago, when standing by poor Henry's bed she had taken it into her hands for the first time and wound it, it had felt cold and heavy. And two days later, when she undid a hook of her crêpe bodice and thrust it inside, it had lain in her bosom like a stone. . . . It had never felt at home there. It's place was — ticking, keeping perfect time, against Henry's firm ribs. It had never trusted her, just as he had never trusted her in those ways. And on the rare occasions when she had forgotten to wind it, she had felt a pang of almost terror, and she had murmured as she fitted the little key: "Forgive me, Henry!"

Old Mrs Travers sighed and pushed the watch under the pillow again. It seemed to her that lately this feeling that it hated her had become more definite. . . . Perhaps that was because she looked at it so often, especially now that she was away from home. Foreign clocks never go. They are always stopped at twenty minutes to two! Such an unpleasant time, neither one thing nor the other. If one arrived anywhere lunch was over and it was too early to expect a cup of tea. . . . But she mustn't begin thinking about tea. Old Mrs Travers pulled herself up in the bed and, like a tired baby, she lifted her arms and let them fall on the eiderdown.

The room was gay with morning light. The big french window on to the balcony was open and the palm outside flung its quivering spider-like shadow over the bedroom walls. Although their hotel did not face the front, at this early hour you could smell the sea, you could hear it breathing, and flying high on golden wings sea-gulls skimmed past. How peaceful the sky looked, as though it was tenderly smiling! Far away — far away from this satin-stripe wall-paper, the glass-covered table, the yellow brocade sofa and chairs, and the mirrors that showed you your side view, your back view, your three-quarters view as well.

Ernestine had been enthusiastic about this room.

"It's just the very room for you, Mother! So bright and attractive and non-depressing! With a balcony, too, so that on wet days you can still have your chair outside and look at those lovely palms. And Gladys can have the little room adjoining, which makes it so beautifully easy for Warner to keep her eye on you both. . . . You couldn't have a nicer room, could you, Mother? I can't get over that sweet balcony! So nice for Gladys! Cecil and I haven't got one at all. . . ."

But all the same, in spite of Ernestine, she never sat on that balcony. For some strange reason that she couldn't explain she hated looking at palms. Nasty foreign things, she called them, in her mind. When they were still they drooped, they looked draggled like immense untidy birds, and when they moved they reminded her always of spiders. Why did they never look just natural and peaceful and shady like English trees? Why were they for ever writhing and twisting or standing sullen? It tried her even to think of them, or in fact of anything foreign. . . .

Honesty

THERE WAS AN EXPRESSION Rupert Henderson was very fond of using: "If you want my *honest* opinion. . . ." He had an honest opinion on every subject under the sun, and nothing short of a passion for delivering it. But Archie Cullen's pet phrase was "I cannot *honestly* say. . . ." Which meant that he had not really made up his mind. He had not really made up his mind on any subject whatsoever. Why? Because he could not. He was unlike other men. He was minus something — or was it plus? No matter. He was not in the least proud of the fact. It depressed him — one might go so far as to say — terribly at times.

Rupert and Archie lived together. That is to say, Archie lived in Rupert's rooms. Oh, he paid his share, his half in everything; the arrangement was a purely, strictly business arrangement. But perhaps it was because Rupert had invited Archie that Archie remained always — his guest. They each had a bedroom — there was a common sitting-room and a largish bathroom which Rupert used as a dressing-room as well. The first morning after his arrival Archie had left his sponge in the bathroom, and a moment after there was a knock at his door and Rupert said, kindly but firmly, "Your sponge, I fancy." The first evening Archie had brought his tobacco jar into the sitting-room and placed it on a corner of the mantelpiece. Rupert was reading the newspaper. It was a round china jar, the surface painted and roughened to represent a sea-urchin. On the lid was a spray of china seaweed with two berries for a knob. Archie was excessively fond of it. But after dinner, when Rupert took out his pipe and pouch, he suddenly fixed his eyes on this object, blew through his moustaches, gasped, and said in a wondering, astonished voice, "I say! Is that yours or Mrs Head's?" Mrs Head was their landlady.

"It's mine," said Archie, and he blushed and smiled just a trifle timidly.

"I *say!*" said Rupert again — this time very meaningly.

"Would you rather I . . ." said Archie, and he moved in his chair to get up.

"No, no! Certainly not! On no account!" answered Rupert, and he actually raised his hand. "But perhaps" — and here he smiled at Archie and gazed about him — "perhaps we might find some spot for it that was a trifle less conspicuous."

The spot was not decided on, however, and Archie nipped his sole personal possession into his bedroom as soon as Rupert was out of the way.

But it was chiefly at meals that the attitude of host and guest was most marked. For instance, on each separate occasion, even before they sat down, Rupert said, "Would you mind cutting the bread, Archie?" Had he not made such a point of it, it is possible that Archie in a moment of abstractedness might have grasped the bread knife. . . . An unpleasant thought! Again, Archie was never allowed to serve. Even at breakfast, the hot dishes and the tea, both were dispensed by Rupert. True, he had half apologised about the tea; he seemed to feel the necessity of some slight explanation, there.

"I'm rather a fad about my tea," said he. "Some people, females especially, pour in the milk first. Fatal habit, for more reasons than one. In my opinion, the cup should be filled just *so* and the tea then coloured. Sugar, Archie?"

"Oh, please," said Archie, almost bowing over the table, Rupert was so very impressive.

"But I suppose," said his friend, "you don't notice any of these little things?"

And Archie answered vaguely, stirring: "No, I don't suppose I do."

Rupert sat down and unfolded his napkin.

"It would be very inconsistent with your character and disposition," said he genially, "if you did! Kidneys and bacon? Scrambled eggs? Either? Both? Which?"

Poor Archie hated scrambled eggs, but, alas! he was practically certain that scrambled eggs were expected of him too. This "psychological awareness", as Rupert called it, which existed between them might after a time make things a trifle difficult. He felt a little abject as he murmured, "Eggs, please." And he saw by Rupert's expression that he had chosen right. Rupert helped him to eggs largely.

II

Psychological awareness . . . perhaps it was that which explained their intimacy. One might have been tempted to say it was a case

126

of mutual fascination. But whereas Archie's reply to the suggestion would have been a slow "Poss-ibly!" Rupert would have flouted it at once.

"Fascination! The word's preposterous in this connection. What on earth would there be in Cullen to fascinate me even if I was in the habit of being fascinated by my fellow creatures; which I certainly am not. No, I'll own I am deeply interested. I confess my belief is, I understand him better than anybody else. And if you want my honest opinion, I am certain that my — my — h'm — influence over — sympathy for — him — call it what you like, is all to the good. There is a psychological awareness. . . . Moreover, as a companion, instinctively I find him extremely agreeable. He stimulates some part of my mind which is less active without him. But fascination — wide of the mark, my dear — wide!"

But supposing one remained unconvinced? Supposing one still played with the idea. Wasn't it possible to see Rupert and Archie as the python and the rabbit keeping house together? Rupert that handsome, well-fed python with his moustaches, his glare, his habit of uncoiling before the fire and swaying against the mantelpiece, pipe and pouch in hand. And Archie, soft, hunched, timid, sitting in the lesser arm-chair, there and not there, flicking back into the darkness at a word but emerging again at a look — with sudden wholly unexpected starts of playfulness (instantly suppressed by the python). Of course, there was no question of anything so crude and dreadful as the rabbit being eaten by his housemate. Nevertheless, it was a strange fact, after a typical evening the one looked immensely swelled, benign and refreshed, and the other, pale, small and exhausted. . . . And more often than not Rupert's final comment was — ominous this — as he doused his whisky with soda:

"This has been very absorbing, Archie." And Archie gasped out, "Oh, *very!*"

III

Archie Cullen was a journalist and the son of a journalist. He had no private money, no influential connections, scarcely any friends. His father had been one of those weak, disappointed, unsuccessful men who see in their sons a weapon for themselves. He would get his own back on life through Archie. Archie would show them the stuff he — his father was made of. Just you wait till my son comes along! This, though highly consoling to Mr Cullen *père*, was terribly poor fun for Archie. At two and a half his infant nose was put to the grindstone and even on Sundays it was not taken off. Then his father took him out walking and improved the occasion by making him spell the shop signs, count the yachts racing in the harbour, divide them by four and multiply the result by three.

But the experiment was an amazing success. Archie turned away from the distractions of life, shut his ears, folded his feet, sat over the table with his book, and when the holidays came he didn't like them; they made him uneasy; so he went on reading for himself. He was a model boy. On prize-giving days his father accompanied him to school, carried the great wad of stiff books home for him and, flinging them on the dining-room table, he surveyed them with an exultant smile. My prizes! The little sacrifice stared at them, too, through his spectacles as other little boys stared at puddings. He ought, of course, at this juncture to have been rescued by a doting mother who, though cowed herself, rose on the . . .

Susannah

OF COURSE there would have been no question of their going to the exhibition if Father had not had the tickets given to him. Little girls cannot expect to be given treats that cost extra money when only to feed them, buy them clothes, pay for their lessons and the house they live in takes their kind generous Father all day and every day working hard from morning till night — "except Saturday afternoons and Sundays," said Susannah.

"Susannah!" Mother was very shocked. "But do you know what would happen to your poor Father if he didn't have a holiday on Saturday afternoons and Sundays?"

"No," said Susannah. She looked interested. "What?"

"He would die," said their Mother impressively.

"Would he?" said Susannah, opening her eyes. She seemed astounded, and Sylvia and Phyllis, who were four and five years older than she, chimed in with "Of course" in a very superior tone. What a little silly-billy she was not to know that! They sounded so convinced and cheerful that their Mother felt a little shaken and hastened to change the subject. . . .

"So that is why," she said a little vaguely, "you must each thank Father separately before you go."

"And then will he give us the money?" asked Phyllis.

"And then I shall ask him for whatever is necessary," said their Mother firmly. She sighed suddenly and got up. "Run along, children, and ask Miss Wade to dress you and get ready herself and then to come down to the dining-room. And now, Susannah, you are not to let go Miss Wade's hand from the moment you are through the gates until you are out again."

"Well — what if I go on a horse?" inquired Susannah.

"Go on a horse — nonsense, child! You're much too young for horses! Only big girls and boys can ride."

"There're roosters for small children," said Susannah, undaunted. "I know, because Irene Heywood went on one and when she got off she fell over."

"All the more reason why you shouldn't go on," said her Mother.

But Susannah looked as though falling over had no terrors for her. On the contrary.

About the exhibition, however, Sylvia and Phyllis knew as little as Susannah. It was the first that had ever come to their town. One morning, as Miss Wade, their lady help, rushed them along to the Heywoods', whose governess they shared, they had seen carts piled with great long planks of wood, sacks, what looked like whole doors, and white flagstaffs, passing through the wide gate of the Recreation Ground. And by the time they were bowled home to their dinners there were the beginnings of a high, thin fence, dotted with flagstaffs, built all round the railings. From inside came a tremendous noise of hammering, shouting, clanging; a little engine, hidden away, went *Chuff-chuff-chuff. Chuff!* And round, woolly balls of smoke were tossed over the palings.

First it was the day after the day after tomorrow, then plain day after tomorrow, then tomorrow, and at last, the day itself. When Susannah woke up in the morning there was a little gold spot of sunlight watching her from the wall; it looked as though it had been there for a long time, waiting to remind her: "It's today — you're going today — this afternoon. Here she is!"

(Second Version)

That afternoon they were allowed to cut jugs and basins out of a draper's catalogue, and at tea-time they had real tea in the doll's tea-set on the table. This was a very nice treat, indeed, except that the doll's teapot wouldn't pour out even after you'd poked a pin down the spout and blown into it.

But the next afternoon, which was Saturday, Father came home in high feather. The front door banged so hard that the whole house shook, and he shouted to Mother from the hall.

"Oh, how more than good of you, darling!" cried Mother, "but how unnecessary too. Of course, they'll simply love it. But to have spent all that money! You shouldn't have done it, Daddy dear! They've totally forgotten all about it. And what is this! Half a crown?" cried Mother. "No! Two shillings, I see," she corrected quickly, "to spend as well. Children! Children! Come down, downstairs!"

Down they came, Phyllis and Sylvia leading, Susannah holding on. "Do you know what Father's done?" And Mother held up her hand. What was she holding? Three cherry tickets and a green one. "He's bought you tickets. You're to go to the exhibition, this very afternoon, all of you, with Miss Wade. What do you say to that?"

"Oh, Mummy! Lovely! Lovely!" cried Phyllis and Sylvia.

"Isn't it?" said Mother. "Run upstairs. Run and ask Miss Wade to get you ready. Don't dawdle. Up you go! All of you."

Away flew Phyllis and Sylvia, but still Susannah stayed where she was at the bottom of the stairs, hanging her head.

"Go along," said Mother. And Father said sharply, "What the devil's the matter with the child?"

Susannah's face quivered. "I don't want to go," she whispered.

"What! Don't want to go to the exhibition! After Father's — You naughty, ungrateful child! Either you go to the exhibition, Susannah, or you will be packed off to bed at once."

Susannah's head bent low, lower still. All her little body bent forward. She looked as though she was going to bow down, to bow down to the ground, before her kind generous Father and beg for his forgiveness. . . .

Second Violin

A FEBRUARY MORNING, windy, cold, with chill-looking clouds hurrying over a pale sky and chill snowdrops for sale in the grey streets. People look small and shrunken as they flit by; they look scared as if they were trying to hide inside their coats from something big and brutal. The shop doors are closed, the awnings are furled, and the policemen at the crossing are lead policemen. Huge empty vans shake past with a hollow sound; and there is a smell of soot and wet stone staircases, a raw, grimy smell. . . .

Flinging her small scarf over her shoulder again, clasping her violin, Miss Bray darts along to orchestra practice. She is conscious of her cold hands, her cold nose and her colder feet. She can't feel her toes at all. Her feet are just little slabs of cold, all of a piece, like the feet of china dolls. Winter is a terrible time for thin people — terrible! Why should it hound them down, fasten on them, worry them so? Why not, for a change, take a nip, take a snap at the fat ones who wouldn't notice? But no! It is sleek, warm, cat-like summer that makes the fat one's life a misery. Winter is all for bones. . . .

Threading her way, like a needle, in and out and along, went Miss Bray, and she thought of nothing but the cold. She had just come out of her kitchen, which was pleasantly snug in the morning, with her gas-fire going for her breakfast and the window closed. She had just drunk three large cups of really boiling tea. Surely, they ought to have warmed her. One always read in books of people going on their way warmed and invigorated by even one cup. And she had had three! How she loved her tea! She was getting fonder and fonder of it. Stirring the cup, Miss Bray looked down. A little fond smile parted her lips, and she breathed tenderly, "I love my tea."

But all the same, in spite of the books, it didn't keep her warm. Cold! Cold! And now as she turned the corner she took such a gulp of damp, cold air that her eyes filled. Yi-yi-yi, a little dog yelped; he looked as though he'd been hurt. She hadn't time to look round, but that high, sharp yelping soothed her, was a comfort even. She could have made just that sound herself.

And here was the Academy. Miss Bray pressed with all her might against the stiff, sulky door, squeezed through into the vestibule hung with pallid notices and concert programmes, and stumbled up the dusty stairs and along the passage to the dressing-room. Through the open door there came such shrill loud laughter, such high, indifferent voices that it sounded like a play going on in there. It was hard to believe people were not laughing and talking like that . . . on purpose. "Excuse me — pardon — sorry," said Miss Bray, nudging her way in and looking quickly round the dingy little room. Her two friends had not yet come.

The First Violins were there; a dreamy, broad-faced girl leaned against her 'cello; two Violas sat on a bench, bent over a music book, and the Harp, a small grey little person, who only came occasionally, leaned against a bench and looked for her pocket in her underskirt. . . .

"I've a run of three twice, ducky," said Ma, "a pair of queens make eight, and one for his nob makes nine."

With an awful hollow groan Alexander, curling his little finger high, pegged nine for Ma. And "Wait now, wait now," said she, and her quick short little hands snatched at the other cards. "My crib, young man!" She spread them out, leaned back, twitched her shawl, put her head on one side. "H'm, not so bad! A flush of four and a pair!"

"Betrayed! Betrayed!" moaned Alexander, bowing his dark head over the cribbage board, "and by a woo-man." He sighed deeply, shuffled the cards and said to Ma, "Cut for me, my love!"

Although, of course, he was only having his joke like all professional young gentlemen, something in the tone in which he said "my love!" gave Ma quite a turn. Her lips trembled as she cut the cards, she felt a sudden pang as she watched those long slim fingers dealing.

Ma and Alexander were playing cribbage in the basement kitchen of number 9 Bolton Street. It was late, it was on eleven, and Sunday night, too — shocking! They sat at the kitchen table that was covered with a worn art serge cloth spotted with candle grease. On one corner of it stood three glasses, three spoons, a saucer of sugar lumps and a bottle of gin. The stove was still alight and the lid of the kettle had just begin to lift, cautiously, stealthily, as though there was someone inside who wanted to have a peep and pop back again. On the horse-hair sofa against the wall by the door the owner of the third glass lay asleep, gently snoring. Perhaps because he had his back to them, perhaps because his feet poked out from the short overcoat covering him, he looked for-lorn, pathetic and the long, fair hair covering his collar looked forlorn and pathetic, too.

"Well, well," said Ma, sighing as she put out two cards and arranged the others in a fan, "such is life. I little thought when I saw the last of you this morning that we'd be playing a game together tonight."

"The caprice of destiny," murmured Alexander. But, as a matter of fact, it was no joking matter. By some infernal mis-chance that morning he and Rinaldo had missed the train that all the company travelled by. That was bad enough. But being Sunday, there was no other train until midnight, and as they had a full rehearsal at ten o'clock on Monday it meant going by that, or getting what the company called the beetroot. But God! what a day it had been. They had left the luggage at the station and come back to Ma's, back to Alexander's frowsy bedroom with the bed unmade and water standing about. Rinaldo had spent the whole day sitting on the side of the bed swinging his leg, dropping ash on the floor and saying, "I wonder what made us lose that train. Strange we should have lost it. I bet the others are wondering what made us lose it, too." And Alexander had stayed by the window gazing into the small garden that was so black with grime even the old lean cat who came and scraped seemed revolted by it, too. It was only after Ma had seen the last of her Sunday visitors . . .

Mr and Mrs Williams

I

THAT WINTER Mr and Mrs Williams of The Rowans, Wicken-ham, Surrey, astonished their friends by announcing that they were going for a three weeks' holiday to Switzerland. Switzerland! How very enterprising and exciting! There was quite a flutter in Wickenham households at the news. Husbands coming home from the city in the evening were greeted immediately with:

"My dear, have you heard the news about the Williams?"

"No! What's up now?"

"They're off to Switzerland."

"Switzerland! What the dickens are they going there for?"

That, of course, was only the extravagance of the moment. One knew perfectly well why people went. But nobody in Wickenham ever plunged so far away from home at that time of year. It was not considered "necessary" — as golf, bridge, a summer holiday at the sea, an account at Harrods' and a small car as soon as one could afford it, were considered necessary. . . .

"Won't you find the initial expenditure very heavy?" asked stout old Mrs Prean, meeting Mrs Williams quite by chance at their nice obliging grocer's. And she brushed the crumbs of a sample cheese biscuit off her broad bosom.

"Oh, we shall get our kit over there," said Mrs Williams.

"Kit" was a word in high favour among the Wickenham ladies. It was left over from the war, of course, with "cheery", "wash-out", "Hun", "Boche", and "Bolshy". As a matter of fact, Bolshy was post-war. But it belonged to the same mood. ("My dear, my house-maid is an absolute little Hun, and I'm afraid the cook is turning Bolshy. . . .") There was a fascination in those words. To use them was like opening one's Red Cross cupboard again and gazing at the remains of the bandages, body-belts, tins of anti-insecticide and so on. One was stirred, one got a far-away thrill, like the thrill of hearing a distant band. It reminded you of those exciting, busy, of course anxious, but tremendous days when the whole of Wickenham was one united family. And, although one's husband was away, one had for a substitute three large photographs of him in uniform. One in a silver frame on the table by the bed, one in the regimental colours on the piano, and one in leather to match the dining-room chairs.

"Cook strongly advised us to buy nothing here," went on Mrs Williams.

"*Cook!*" cried Mrs Prean, greatly astounded. "What can —"

"Oh — *Thomas* Cook, of course, I mean," said Mrs Williams, smiling brightly. Mrs Prean subsided.

"But you will surely not depend upon the resources of a little Swiss village for clothes?" she persisted, deeply interested, as usual, in other people's affairs.

"Oh no, certainly not." Mrs Williams was quite shocked. "We shall get all we need in the way of clothes from Harrods'."

That was what Mrs Prean had wished to hear. That was as it should be.

"The great secret, my dear" (she always knew the great secret), "the great secret" — and she put her hand on Mrs Williams' arm and spoke very distinctly — "is plenty of long-sleeved woven combies!"

"Thank you, m'm."

Both ladies started. There at their side was Mr Wick, the nice grocer, holding Mrs Prean's parcel by a loop of pink string. Dear me — how very awkward! He must have . . . he couldn't possibly not have. . . . In the emotion of the moment Mrs Prean, thinking to gloss it over tactfully, nodded significantly at Mrs Williams and said, accepting the parcel, "And that is what I always tell my dear son!" But this was too swift for Mrs Williams to follow.

Her embarrassment continued and, ordering the sardines, she just stopped herself from saying "Three large pairs, Mr Wick, please," instead of "Three large tins."

II

As a matter of fact it was Mrs Williams' Aunt Aggie's happy release which had made their scheme possible. Happy release it was! After fifteen years in a wheel-chair passing in and out of the little house at Ealing she had, to use the nurse's expression, "just glided away at the last". Glided away . . . it sounded as thought Aunt Aggie had taken the wheel-chair with her. One saw her, in her absurd purple velvet, steering carefully among the stars and whimpering faintly, as was her terrestrial wont, when the wheel jolted over a particularly large one.

Aunt Aggie had left her dear niece Gwendolen two hundred and fifty pounds. Not a vast sum by any means but quite a nice little windfall. Gwendolen in that dashing mood that only women know, decided immediately to spend it — part of it on the house and the rest on a treat for Gerald. And the lawyer's letter happening to come at tea-time together with a copy of the *Sphere* full of the most fascinating, thrilling photographs of holiday-makers at Mürren and St Moritz and Montana, the question of the treat was settled.

"You would like to go to Switzerland, wouldn't you, Gerald?"

"Very much."

"You're — awfully good at skating and all that kind of thing — aren't you?"

"Fairly."

"You do feel it's a thing to be done — don't you?"

"How do you mean?"

But Gwendolen only laughed. That was so like Gerald. She knew, in his heart of hearts, he was every bit as keen as she was. But he had this horror of showing his feelings — like all men. Gwendolen understood it perfectly and wouldn't have had him different for the world. . . .

"I'll write to Cook's at once and tell them we don't want to go to a very fashionable place and we don't want one of those big jazzy hotels! I'd much prefer a really small out-of-the-way place where we could really go in for the sports seriously." This was quite untrue, but, like so many of Gwendolen's statements, it was made to please Gerald. "Don't you agree?"

Gerald lit his pipe for reply.

As you have gathered, the Christian names of Mr and Mrs Williams were Gwendolen and Gerald. How well they went together! They sounded married. Gwendolen-Gerald. Gwendolen wrote them, bracketed, on bits of blotting-paper, on the backs of old envelopes, on the Stores' catalogue. They looked married. Gerald, when they were on their honeymoon, had made an awfully good joke about them. He had said one morning, "I say, has it ever struck you that both our names begin with G? Gwendolen-Gerald. You're a G," and he had pointed his razor at her — he was shaving — "and I'm a G. Two Gs. Gee-Gee. See?"

Oh, Gwendolen saw immediately. It was really most witty. Quite brilliant! And so — sweet and unexpected of him to have thought of it. Gee-Gee. Oh, *very* good! She wished she could have told it to people. She had an idea that some people thought Gerald had not a very strong sense of humour. But it was a little too intimate. All the more precious for that reason, however.

"My dear, did you think of it at this moment? I mean — did you just make it up on the spot?"

Gerald, rubbing the lather with a finger, nodded. "Flashed into my mind while I was soaping my face," said he seriously. "It's a queer thing" — and he dipped the razor into the pot of hot water — "I've noticed it before. Shaving gives me ideas." It did, indeed, thought Gwendolen. . . .

Weak Heart

ALTHOUGH IT SOUNDED all the year round, although it rang out sometimes as early as half-past six in the morning, sometimes as late as half-past ten at night, it was in the spring, when Bengel's violet patch just inside the gate was blue with flowers, that that piano . . . made the passers-by not only stop talking, but slow down, pause, look suddenly — if they were men — grave, even stern, and if they were women — dreamy, even sorrowful.

Tarana Street was beautiful in the spring; there was not a single house without its garden and trees and a plot of grass big enough to be called "the lawn". Over the low painted fences, you could see, as you ran by, whose daffys were out, whose wild snowdrop border was over and who had the biggest hyacinths, so pink and white, the colour of coconut ice. But nobody had violets that grew, that smelled in the spring sun like Bengel's. Did they really smell like that? Or did you shut your eyes and lean over the fence because of Edie Bengel's piano?

A little wind ruffles among the leaves like a joyful hand looking for the finest flowers; and the piano sounds gay, tender, laughing. Now a cloud, like a swan, flies across the sun, the violets shine cold, like water, and a sudden questioning cry rings from Edie Bengel's piano.

. . . Ah, if life must pass so quickly, why is the breath of these flowers so sweet? What is the meaning of this feeling of longing, of sweet trouble — of flying joy? Good-bye! Farewell! The young bees lie half awake on the slender dandelions, silver are the pink-tipped arrowy petals of the daisies; the new grass shakes in the light. Everything is beginning again, marvellous as ever, heavenly fair. "Let me stay! Let me stay!" pleads Edie Bengel's piano.

It is the afternoon, sunny and still. The blinds are down in the front to save the carpets, but upstairs the slats are open and in the golden light little Mrs Bengel is feeling under her bed for the square bonnet box. She is flushed. She feels timid, excited, like a girl. And now the tissue paper is parted, her best bonnet, the one trimmed with a jet butterfly, which reposes on top, is lifted out and solemnly blown upon.

Dipping down to the glass she tries it with fingers that tremble. She twitches her dolman round her slender shoulders, clasps her purse and before leaving the bedroom kneels down a moment to ask God's blessing on her "goings out". And as she kneels there quivering, she is rather like a butterfly herself, fanning her wings before her Lord. When the door is open the sound of the piano coming up through the silent house is almost frightening, so bold, so defiant, so reckless it rolls under Edie's fingers. And just for a moment the thought comes to Mrs Bengel and is gone again, that there is a stranger with Edie in the drawing-room, but a fantastic person, out of a book, a — a — villain. It's very absurd. She flits across the hall, turns the door handle and confronts her flushed daughter. Edie's hands drop from the keys. She squeezes them between her knees, her head is bent, her curls are fallen forward. She gazes at her mother with brilliant eyes. There is something painful in that glance, something very strange. It is dusky in the drawing-room, the top of the piano is open. Edie has been playing from memory, it's as though the air still tingles.

"I'm going, dear," said Mrs Bengel softly, so softly it is like a sigh.

"Yes, Mother," came from Edie.

"I don't expect I shall be long."

Mrs Bengel lingers. She would very much like just a word of sympathy, of understanding, even from Edie, to cheer her on her way.

But Edie murmurs, "I'll put the kettle on in half an hour."

"Do, dear!" Mrs Bengel grasped at that even. A nervous little smile touched her lips. "I expect I shall want my tea."

But to that Edie makes no reply; she frowns, she stretches out a hand, quickly unscrews one of the piano candlesticks, lifts off a pink china ring and screws all tight again. The ring has been rattling. As the front door bangs softly after her mother Edie and the piano seem to plunge together into deep dark water, into waves that flow over both, relentless. She plays on desperately until her nose is white and her heart beats. It is her way of getting over her nervousness and her way too of praying. Would they accept her? Would she be allowed to go? Was it possible that in a week's time she would be one of Miss Farmer's girls, wearing a red and blue hat-band, running up the broad steps leading to the big grey painted house that buzzed, that hummed as you went by? Their pew in church faced Miss Farmer's boarders. Would she at last know the names of the girls she had looked at so often? The pretty pale one with red hair, the dark one with a fringe, the fair one who held Miss Farmer's hand during the sermon? . . . But after all . . .

It was Edie's fourteenth birthday. Her father gave her a silver brooch with a bar of music, two crotchets, two quavers and a minim headed by a very twisted treble clef. Her mother gave her blue satin gloves and two boxes for gloves and handkerchiefs, hand-painted the glove box with a sprig of gold roses tying up the capital G and the handkerchief box with a marvellously lifelike butterfly quivering on the capital H. From the aunts in . . .

There was a tree at the corner of Tarana Street and May Street. It grew so close to the pavement that the heavy boughs stretched over, and on that part of the pavement there was always a fine sifting of minute twigs.

But in the dusk, lovers parading came into its shade as into a tent. There, however long they had been together, they greeted each other again with long kisses, with embraces that were sweet torture, agony to bear, agony to end.

Edie never knew that Roddie "loved" it, Roddie never knew that it meant anything to Edie.

Roddie, spruce, sleek with water, bumped his new bike down the wooden steps, through the gate. He was off for a spin, and looking at that tree, dark in the glow of evening, he felt the tree was watching him. He wanted to do marvels, to astonish, to shock, to amaze it.

Roddie had a complete new outfit for the occasion. A black serge suit, a black tie, a straw hat so white it was almost silver, a dazzling white straw hat with a broad black band. Attached to the hat there was a thick guard that somehow reminded one of a fishing line and the little clasp on the brim was like a fly. . . . He stood at the graveside, his legs apart, his hands loosely clasped, and watched Edie being lowered into the grave — as a half-grown boy watches anything, a man at work, or a bicycle accident, or a chap cleaning a spring-carriage wheel — but suddenly as the men drew back he gave a violent start, turned, muttered something to his father and dashed away, so fast that people looked positively frightened, through the cemetery, down the avenue of dripping clay banks into Tarana Road, and started pelting for home. His suit was very tight and hot. It was like a dream. He kept his head down and his fists clenched, he couldn't look up, nothing could have made him look higher than the tops of the fences — What was he thinking of as he pressed along? On, on until the gate was reached, up the steps, in at the front door, through the hall, up to the drawing-room.

"Edie!" called Roddie. "Edie, old girl!"

And he gave a low strange squawk and cried "Edie!" and stared across at Edie's piano.

But cold, solemn, as if frozen, heavily the piano stared back at Roddie. Then it answered, but on its own behalf, on behalf of the house and the violet patch, the garden, the velvet tree at the corner of May Street, and all that was delightful: "There is nobody here of that name, young man!"

Widowed

THEY CAME DOWN to breakfast next morning absolutely their own selves. Rosy, fresh, and just chilled enough by the cold air blowing through the bedroom windows to be very ready for hot coffee.

"Nippy." That was Geraldine's word as she buttoned on her orange coat with pink-washed fingers. "Don't you find it decidedly nippy?" And her voice, so matter-of-fact, so natural, sounded as though they had been married for years.

Parting his hair with two brushes (marvellous feat for a woman to watch) in the little round mirror, he had replied, lightly clapping the brushes together, "My dear, have you got enough *on*?" and he, too, sounded as though well he knew from the experience of years her habit of clothing herself underneath in wisps of chiffon and two satin bows. . . . Then they ran down to breakfast, laughing together and terribly startling the shy parlour-maid who, after talking it over with Cook, had decided to be invisible until she was rung for.

"Good morning, Nellie, I think we shall want more toast than *that*," said the smiling Geraldine as she hung over the breakfast table. She deliberated — "Ask Cook to make us four more pieces, please."

Marvellous, the parlour-maid thought it was. And as she closed the door she heard the voice say, "I do so hate to be short of toast, don't you?"

He was standing in the sunny window. Geraldine went up to him. She put her hand on his arm and gave it a gentle squeeze. How pleasant it was to feel that rough man's-tweed again. Ah, how pleasant! She rubbed her hand against it, touched it with her cheek, sniffed the smell.

The window looked out on to flower beds, a tangle of Michaelmas daisies, late dahlias, hanging heavy, and shaggy little asters. Then there came a lawn strewn with yellow leaves with a broad path beyond and a row of gold-fluttering trees. An old gardener, in woollen mitts, was sweeping the path, brushing the leaves into a neat little heap. Now, the broom tucked in his arm, he fumbled in his coat pocket, brought out some matches, and scooping a hole in the leaves he set fire to them.

Such lovely blue smoke came breathing into the air through those dry leaves; there was something so calm and orderly in the way the pile burned that it was a pleasure to watch. The old gardener stumped away and came back with a handful of withered twigs. He flung them on and stood by, and little light flames began to flicker.

"I do think," said Geraldine, "I do think there is nothing nicer than a real satisfactory fire."

"Jolly, isn't it," he murmured back, and they went to their first breakfast.

Just over a year ago, thirteen months, to be exact, she had been standing before the dining-room window of the little house in Sloane Street. It looked over the railed gardens. Breakfast was over, cleared away and done with . . . she had a fat bunch of letters in her hand that she meant to answer, snugly, over the fire. But before settling down, the autumn sun, the freshness had drawn her to the window. Such a perfect morning for the Row. Jimmie had gone riding.

"Good-bye, dear thing."

"Good-bye, Gerry mine." And then the morning kiss, quick and firm. He looked so handsome in his riding kit. She imagined him as she stood there . . . riding. Geraldine was not very good at imagining things. But there was a mist, a thud of hooves and Jimmie's moustache was damp. From the garden there sounded the creak of a gardener's barrow. An old man came into sight with a load of leaves and a broom lying across. He stopped; he began to sweep. "What enormous tufts of irises grew in London gardens," mused Geraldine. "Why?" And now the smoke of a real fire ascended.

"There is nothing nicer," she thought, "than a really satisfactory fire."

Just at that moment the telephone bell rang. Geraldine sat down at Jimmie's desk to answer it. It was Major Hunter.

"Good morning, Major. You're a very early bird!"

"Good morning, Mrs Howard. Yes. I am." (Geraldine made a little surprised face at herself. How odd he sounded!) "Mrs Howard, I'm coming round to see you . . . now. . . . I'm taking a taxi. . . . Please don't go out. And — and —" the voice stammered, "p-please don't let the servants go out."

"*Par*-don?" this last was so very peculiar, though the whole thing had been peculiar enough, that Geraldine couldn't believe what she heard. But he was gone. He had rung off. What on earth — and putting down the receiver, she took up a pencil and drew what she always drew when she sat down before a piece of blotting-paper — the behind of a little cat with whiskers and tail complete. Geraldine must have drawn that little cat hundreds of times, all over the the world, in hotels, in clubs, at steamer desks, waiting at the bank. The little cat was her sign, her mark. She had copied it from a little girl at school when she thought it most wonderful. And she never tried anything else. She was . . . not very good at drawing. This particular cat was drawn with an extra firm pen and even its whiskers looked surprised.

"Not to let the servants go out!" But she had never heard anything so peculiar in her life. She must have made a mistake. Geraldine couldn't help a little giggle of amusement. And why should he tell her he was taking a taxi? And why — above all — should he be coming to see her at that hour of the morning?

Then — it came over her — like a flash she remembered Major Hunter's mania for old furniture. They had been discussing it at the Carlton the last time they lunched together. And he had said something to Jimmie about some — Jacobean or Queen Anne — Geraldine knew nothing about these things — something or other. Could he possibly be bringing it round? But of course. He must be. And that explained the remark about the servants. He wanted them to help getting it into the house. What a bore! Geraldine did hope it would tone in. And really, she must say she thought Major Hunter was taking a good deal for granted to produce a thing that size at that hour of the day without a word of warning. They hardly knew him well enough for that. Why make such a mystery of it too? Geraldine hated mysteries. But she had heard his head was rather troublesome at times ever since the Somme affair. Perhaps this was one of his bad days. In that case, a pity Jimmie was not back. She rang. Mullins answered.

"Oh, Mullins, I'm expecting Major Hunter in a few moments. He's bringing something rather heavy. He may want you to help with it. And Cook had better be ready too."

Geraldine's manner was slightly lofty with her servants. She enjoyed carrying things off with a high hand. All the same, Mullins did look surprised. She seemed to hover for a moment before she went out. It annoyed Geraldine greatly. What was there to be surprised at? What could have been simpler? she thought, sitting down to her batch of letters, and the fire, and the clock and her pen began to whisper together.

There was the taxi — making an enormous noise at the door. She thought she heard the driver's voice too, arguing. It took her a long moment to clasp her writing-case and to get up out of the low chair. The bell rang. She went straight to the dining-room door —

And there was Major Hunter in his riding kit, coming quickly towards her, and behind him, through the open door at the bottom of the steps, she saw something big, something grey. It was an ambulance.

"There's been an accident," cried Geraldine sharply.

"Mrs Howard." Major Hunter ran forward. He put out his icy cold hand and wrung hers. "You'll be brave, won't you?" he said, he pleaded.

But of course she would be brave.

"Is it serious?"

Major Hunter nodded gravely. He said the one word "Yes."

"Very serious?"

Now he raised his head. He looked her full in the eyes. She'd never realised until that moment that he was extraordinarily handsome though in a melodrama kind of way. "It's as bad as it can be, Mrs Howard," said Major Hunter simply. "But — go in there," he said hastily, and he almost pushed her into her own dining-room. "We must bring him in — where can we —"

"Can he be taken upstairs?" asked Geraldine.

"Yes, yes, of course." Major Hunter looked at her so strangely — so painfully.

"There's his dressing-room," said Geraldine. "It's on the first floor. I'll lead the way," and she put her hand on the Major's arm. "It's quite all right, Major," she said, "I'm not going to break down —" and she actually smiled, a confident brilliant smile.

To her amazement, as Major Hunter turned away he burst out with, "Ah, my God! I'm so sorry."

Poor man. He was quite overcome. "Brandy afterwards," thought Geraldine. "Not now, of course."

It was a painful moment when she heard those measured deliberate steps in the hall. But Geraldine, realising this was not the moment, and there was nothing to be gained by it, refrained from looking.

"This way, Major." She skimmed on in front, up the stairs, along the passage; she flung open the door of Jimmie's gay, living, breathing dressing-room and stood to one side — for Major Hunter, for the two stretcher-bearers. Only then she realised that it must be a scalp wound — some injury to the head. For there was nothing to be seen of Jimmie; the sheet was pulled right over. . . .

SELECT BIBLIOGRAPHY

Katherine Mansfield:

In a German Pension. London, Stephen Swift, December 1911.

Prelude. Richmond, Hogarth Press, July 1918.

Je ne parle pas français. Hampstead, Heron Press, February 1920.

Bliss and Other Stories. London, Constable, December 1920.

The Garden-Party and Other Stories. London, Constable,
February 1922.

The Doves' Nest and Other Stories, ed. J. M. Murry. London,
Constable, June 1923.

Something Childish and Other Stories, ed. J. M. Murry. London,
Constable, August 1924.

The Aloe, ed. J. M. Murry. London, Constable, 1930.

The Letters of Katherine Mansfield, ed. J. M. Murry, 2 vols. London,
Constable, 1928.

Katherine Mansfield's Letters to John Middleton Murry, 1913–1922,
ed. J. M. Murry. London, Constable, 1951.

Journal of Katherine Mansfield, "Definitive Edition",
ed. J. M. Murry. London, Constable, 1954.

The Urewera Notebook, ed. I. A. Gordon. Wellington, O.U.P., 1978.

The Collected Letters of Katherine Mansfield, ed. V. O'Sullivan and
M. Scott. Vols I and II. Oxford, Clarendon Press, 1984, 1987.

Alpers, Anthony. *The Life of Katherine Mansfield*. London, Cape,
1980.

Baker, Ida. *Katherine Mansfield: The Memories of L.M.*
London, Michael Joseph, 1971.

Hankin, C. A. *Katherine Mansfield and Her Confessional Stories*.
London, Macmillan, 1983.

Hankin, C. A. (ed.). *The Letters of John Middleton Murry to
Katherine Mansfield*. London, Constable, 1983.

Mantz, Ruth Elvish, and J. M. Murry. *The Life of Katherine
Mansfield*. London, Constable, 1933.

Murry, J. M. *Between Two Worlds, an Autobiography*. London, Cape,
1935.

Woolf, Virginia. *The Diary of Virginia Woolf*, ed. Anne Olivier Bell.
Vols I and II. London, Hogarth Press, 1977, 1978.